# Eve's Rib

## Diane Hanger

*Dear Tony,*

*You really are my treasured family!*

*Love and Aloha!*

*Diane*

outskirtspress

DENVER, COLORADO

Outskirts Press, Inc.
http://www.outskirtspress.com

ISBN: 978-1-4327-9756-0

Outskirts Press and the "OP" logo are trademarks belonging to Outskirts Press, Inc.

*During the journey of writing, editing and finally publishing this book, my husband Bruce, and my daughters, Valerie, Jessica, Cynthia and Lucinda, have given constant support. Others in the family have contributed also, and all have patiently read and critiqued the manuscript, always cheering me on. No words can express my thanks. I've done it for you.*

*Chapter One*

# Sunday

**Airplanes do not** play favorites. The grieving passenger on his way to a funeral is moved along at the same rate of speed as the soldier-hero returning to a glorious homecoming. The exuberant young woman flying to Barcelona for her exotic wedding is seated next to the heartsick young wife leaving her failed marriage behind.

On this flight, amid the sea of happy faces, three women lacked any glow of excitement, exhibiting no sign of anticipation for what lay ahead. Allison sat in quiet determination, gazing quietly out the window. Toward the rear of the plane, Susan sat with a dull, reconciled demeanor, too weary to care. Midway, in an aisle seat, almost visible emotional chains shackled Glynnis, as she seemed to be hurtled helplessly toward her destination, straining toward the center aisle to avoid any glimpse of the view from the plane window.

For hours the 747 flew relentlessly over the mirror of Pacific Ocean, and then at last it skimmed the Windward coast of Oahu, the ancient Koolau Mountains rising from the sea in misty, mystic welcome. Then it skimmed Diamond Head, Waikiki Beach, with its crystal blue-green water and romantic palm trees. Paradise beckoned all those aboard Flight 136 to shed their troubles and relax in its tropical loveliness, to drink in the heady Island perfume of her vivid blossoms in ultimate surrender to her beauty.

Passengers stirred in their seats, shifting to get a glimpse, a first moment of stolen pleasure. Cameras clicked. The volume of the chatter accelerated a notch with excitement. But three sat with their private thoughts, unmoved.

*I can't believe this is happening*, mused Allison as she marveled at the turquoise water below. *Wouldn't you know it? A dream coming true, and I'm here alone, no Joe sitting next to me, no kids going at it about who sits next to the window. This isn't how it should be.* She laughed to herself. *But hey, maybe it's not how you'd dreamed it would be, but this is it, take it or leave it. Let's not waste the money it took to get here regretting something you can't change.* She laughed at the irony of it. *No, whatever you do, don't throw a wet blanket on the whole trip just because your life is crumbling right before your eyes! Definitely wouldn't fit your 'so-very-nice' personality!* Allison could feel anger and frustration taking control, and she instinctively reigned in on her emotions, took several deep breaths and tapped her finger. Any one of her friends or family would recognize this as her get-it-together mode. They knew that when the drumming eventually stopped, they would see a mischievous smile on her face, the dead giveaway that her indomitable sense of humor had overcome the worry or anger. Her scowl was gone, the smile firmly in place. *And anyhow, if you weren't about to land in this beautiful, sunny place, you'd be shoveling snow out of the driveway, hauling wood for the stove, and trying to locate mittens and hats for those two sweet kids before the school bus clattered down the road. Face up to it. Anybody leaving Homer, Alaska in mid-February to kick off their shoes and walk barefoot in the warm sands of Waikiki doesn't deserve too much sympathy. So buck up, girl, treat your fish-white skin to some sun, and enjoy, at least a little.*

Allison Bradley's numerous friends loved her because she was down-home honest. It was her nature to work with life as it was dealt out without worrying too much about the why-me's and what-if's along the way. 'Unflappable' was the word her best friend Joyce used to describe Allie. However, in these last months she'd felt the sturdy fabric of her marriage unraveling, and couldn't comprehend what had happened, let alone how to repair it. So here she was, sitting on a plane heading for a solitary stay in Hawaii to sort things out. Her calmness and control had been strained to the hilt. Maybe getting away from the center of her troubles and taking this trip would allow her some relaxed and unfettered time to think clearly and find a solution that would restore her normal happy life. Maybe.

Wriggling out from her window seat, Allison maneuvered down the aisle to the bathroom to freshen up. She splashed cold water on her face to shake off the drowsiness brought on by so many hours in a confining space. Patting away the water, she took a long look at herself in the small mirror, smiling and nodding at the familiar image. *Same old me. Funny how used to yourself you get. Always wondered if I see the same face that others see. Maybe I'm really ravishing in other's eyes. Or really ugly! Nobody is ever going to launch a thousand ships because of my face, I do know that. But I guess I'm okay. At least consistent—brown hair, but not mousy brown; pretty good complexion, even though I don't get enough sun to get a tan. But working outdoors a lot has made my skin healthy, if a little faded out and dry. Mom was kind enough to pass along her pretty green eyes. Joe says these eyes caught him the first time he looked at me and he could never get away!* Her shoulders slumped a little and she sighed. *Joe. Whatever has happened to us?* She shrugged and raised her eyebrows. *Okay, troops, enough of this, it's time to land. Maybe the romantic trade winds will clear out the cobwebs in my head and I'll do some useful thinking for a change. Hawaii, do your stuff!*

Waikiki's beauty was not new to Susan. She couldn't recall the first trip to Hawaii; she'd been no more than a toddler. Although her parents didn't make a yearly trip, they normally stayed a month every other year. Growing up in California's crown jewel, Carmel-by-the-Sea, cradled by the ease and lazy happiness that came with her architect father's successful career there, she chided her mother and father once about their senseless flight from one dream location to another, just for a change of scene. Mother had laughed in agreement, but added, "Everyone has their own tolerance level for fog, Susan, and mine is pushed to its maximum every morning when I look out and see that gray blanket covering our beautiful view of the ocean. And your father might love the fog, but consider the ocean temperature. For a college swimmer of some note, Carmel does not afford him much activity. He needs a little time in the tropics now and then to play the fish." Susan had reminded her that in Carmel's early artist colony, Bohemian days, author James Hopper had swum daily in the cold waters, strong and stoic. "Ah, but Susan, your father's not heroic when it comes to water temperature. He likes his ocean warm and full of tropical fishes!" And so the visits to the Islands were a part of her youth.

After law school, when her income grew handsomely as a trial lawyer in the top San Francisco firm of Atchison,

Boardman & McCullough, Susan could have continued the pattern of vacations, but there was never time. She worked 16-hour days, slept with a yellow legal pad near her pillow, resisted involvement with men, although she'd had three romantic involvements. Philip Alexander had been the last, and serious, attachment. To her friends it was obvious that he and Susan were perfect for one another, a romantic "10" that also made good sense, and they watched and nodded like delighted matchmakers as the couple moved happily toward a more solid commitment. But with serious consideration of marriage, they discovered a major roadblock. The ensuing months were stormy and the couple's relationship floundered. Susan was in the unfamiliar position of being totally unable to improve the situation. The combination of a final, wrenching parting with Philip and her near-collapse from working through a devastating crisis at the office allowed her only a scattered few hours of fretful sleep at night and left her without energy or ideas. The firm had narrowly escaped losing their premier client because of sloppy work by one of the firm's attorneys, and she'd been instrumental in salvaging the account. "You managed to put Humpty-Dumpty back together again, Sue-Babe," the managing partner told her in rare praise. But when it was over, she was so exhausted and burned out, she'd come close to throwing in the towel and dumping everything that she'd struggled for. Getting away to regain her strength and composure or face losing everything was a hard, but logical, decision, and Susan lived by logic. And so she grudgingly conceded that this time she considered 'frittered away' vacationing was preferable to abandoning the ten years she'd spent positioning herself in the firm.

The blue and green scene passed her window without much notice. She was tired. She just wanted to land, find a warm beach and close her eyes.

Glynnis Paxton fidgeted nervously in her aisle seat, trying not to look toward any window. Terrifying thoughts ran through her head. *I don't think I'm going to like this landing. Taking off was terrible, and this looks worse. A tiny landing strip surrounded by ocean.* She shuddered. *I'll never understand why Uncle John insisted I do this, and I can't believe I agreed to it, even with him twisting my arm. There's so much to do at home and no conceivable reason for me to be here. I know not one soul on this Island. What happens if I lose my wallet or airplane ticket or hotel key? I'm not going to be a baby and call John all the time, but I don't know a thing about this place. I might get lost in the worst part of town. Could I call a taxi? It might not be a wise choice here. Who knows, the driver could be a hoodlum. Oh please God, help me get through this.* As the panic started to grab her chest, Glynnis had the feeling the other passengers could see right through the outer composure that she hoped she exhibited into her deep fear of being alone in a strange place for the first time. *It's my own fault. How could I be well into my 30s and still jump at my own shadow!* Glynnis sadly acknowledged how, without making a clear decision to do it, she'd thrown away the chance for a life of her own in favor of the safer, very responsible but non-threatening duty of caring for her elderly parents. Now they were gone, and she was a 36-year-old fledgling tottering on the edge of the nest, afraid to fly for the first time.

As they did unconsciously so many times each day, her hands performed a careful inspection of her face and clothing, assuring Glynnis everything was in place and tidy. Nervously, but with the strength and grace born of years of piano study, her long fingers searched for stray wisps of fawn-toned hair to weave back into a thick, expertly plaited French braid looped into a bun. Satisfied with the hair, the hands moved to inspect her face, perhaps suspecting they would find a bead of nervous perspiration. They passed around her gray eyes and pressed down over her temples, then over the delicate nose to massage high cheekbones, trailing down gently to cup around a slender neck. Straightening slightly, Glynnis grasped the edges of the collar of her white blouse, turning it up and re-folding it with precision over her navy blue linen jacket. She sighed quietly. She'd done everything possible to make herself ready to exit the plane, but knew she was far from ready to do so.

Stewardesses patrolled the aisles efficiently, picking up cups and glasses and preparing the plane for landing. Pearl Harbor appeared and the plane banked toward the ground.

"Well, folks, we'll be landing at Honolulu International Airport in just a few seconds. Please remain seated until the plane has come to a full stop. We hope your stay is as wonderful as you've dreamed it would be. Thanks for traveling with Inter-World, and we hope you'll fly with us again when you want to return to this Magic Island." The pilot's words gave official sanction to let the holidays begin, and passengers prepared to do just that. Except Allison, who drew a deep, determined breath, Susan, who simply waited, and Glynnis, who nervously braced herself.

The first thing Allison experienced as she deboarded was the incredibly balmy air carrying delicious, sweet fragrances on the gentle trade winds, heavy with humidity. Even when she and the other passengers entered the airport it was as though they remained outside since most of the structure was open to the elements. Faces were smiling, relaxed. Everyone dressed to accommodate the climate—men wore Aloha shirts in a kaleidoscope of colors and designs, and women were comfortably dressed in either shorts, light slacks, or muu-muus, the full-length, loose dress that was a legacy from the Calvinistic influence of the 1800s.

At this time of year, Alaska was monochromatic. Allison loved it, the wet black of ground, rock and tree contrasting with white snow uncorrupted by encroaching humanity. The stark reality of winter created a severe, unflinching beauty. It was breathtaking, to be sure, awesome. But at the same time there was an awareness of life's uncertainties and the unrelenting forces of nature that were beyond one's control. You were humbled by this beauty, even as you marveled at its magnificence.

The colors of Hawaii were more vibrant than any she had seen before. Poster paint colors. The blue sky provided a tropical canvas for the lush green leaves and exotic crimsons, golds, oranges of the flowers that were so lavishly strewn everywhere you looked. The white blossoms had none of the cold bite of snow, they held a warm sensuality. Somehow these hues possessed such depth, so much life. That was it, she realized. Hawaii was set on a stage of living color.

Allison turned to the woman she'd spoken with briefly as they'd stood next to one another in the aisle of the plane waiting for the doors to open a few moments earlier. Her heart had gone out to this timid lady who looked so terrified.

After a brief conversation, she had more or less glued herself near Allison, not speaking any more or asking for help, but obviously happier having a pilot to guide her through the airport.

"Isn't this terrific? I never thought I'd ever really get here. It's just like a picture postcard, isn't it?" Allison's voice left no doubt about her excitement.

"Oh, of course. I certainly never expected to be here, either." Glynnis spoke with measured enthusiasm, her voice belying her fear. Without doubt, she never dreamed she'd be here, and it took monumental courage to keep going. What a help it was to be able to latch on behind someone who had at least smiled at her and seemed friendly. "I'm sorry, my name is Glynnis Paxton. This is my first airplane trip—in fact, it's the first time I've been very far from home, so I'm a little edgy about everything. I'm not sophisticated about travel. And I very much appreciate your kindness. I didn't think I'd be talking to anyone for the next two weeks!

"Hi, Glynnis. It's really nice to know you. I'm Allison. Allison Bradley. Hey, this is my first trip to Hawaii, too. I've traveled a bit, but it's still pretty exciting for me to get on a plane and take off for a new place."

There was a touch of envy in Glynnis' voice as she answered. "But you make it sound like an adventure. I'm thinking of it more as a prison sentence!"

"Well, y'know, every day of my life is an adventure! Two weeks ago I had to scare a bear out of the yard so the kids could go to school, so I think I can handle Paradise! I hope you really enjoy your stay here. Who knows, it may be the only time you ever get here. 'Let it enchant you,' like they say in the travel brochures!" Allison hoped a light touch might help. "By the way,

I hope we're headed in the right direction for baggage. I'm just following the crowd. Somebody here must know the way."

They passed a lei stand, and Allison impulsively stepped over to the diminutive, dark-haired Hawaiian lady behind the stand. Surrounded by a sea of flower leis, she was industriously stringing white carnation blossoms and sprigs of fern in yet another work of art.

"I'd like two leis, please. Two of the most fragrant ones you have. They're for my friend and me, to celebrate our first visit."

"Get the ginger leis, yeah? Make you think you were born right here in Hawaii." When this lady said 'Hawaii,' there was a fluidity to the word, a faint 'v' instead of the 'w', and a catch in her throat as she ended the word—Hava-i'i.

Allison liked this beautiful Hawaiian lady and loved what she heard, even though it made her own voice sound flat and brassy in contrast as she replied. "That's just what I'll do. This will start our vacations off perfectly. Thanks. What is your name?"

"Malia." The lei-maker smiled with her whole face.

Allison returned the smile as she paid for the flowers.

"Mahalo—thank you." Malia took one of the leis and put it over Allison's head, kissing her cheek as she did so. "Aloha. Enjoy our lovely land."

"Couldn't you get to love this, Glynnis?" Allison was beaming as she returned to her companion's side. "Aloha. Enjoy this lovely land!" She slipped the second lei over Glynnis' head as she repeated the lei-maker's words, and with a smile she, too, accompanied the flowers with a kiss.

Glynnis was overcome. "How very sweet you are. This is beautiful. Nothing like this has ever happened to me before!

It's almost like reading a novel: 'Young Pennsylvania wallflow-er finds herself in Paradise and the friendliness of the Islands comes true for her.' Imagine, being given a lei in welcome."

"You see, it's not that hard to relax and enjoy. Look, here we are at the baggage carousel."

As beautiful as the surroundings were, the damp heat was tiring to the newcomers, and both girls hoped their luggage would show up among the first pieces on the carousel. Glynnis dabbed her face with a handkerchief and shifted her feet, wish-ing she'd bought some comfortable sandals. Nylon stockings and pumps were not a good choice, even though she'd tried to dress for a tropical vacation. She'd chosen nude-colored ny-lons, which seemed appropriate for hot weather and the shoes were sensibly low-heeled. But obviously Glynnis didn't know much about the tropics. Her first purchase would be sandals. And she'd throw away the nylons!

Allison was warm, but more relaxed. She'd worn her fa-vorite Levi's and a soft cotton blouse. The down jacket and snow boots worn to the airport in Anchorage in -20 degree weather had been stowed in a locker there, awaiting her re-turn, when she'd surely need them again. Right now, they were the furthest things from her mind.

Nearby, Susan was met by a driver from the vacation com-plex where she would be staying in her parents' condominium. Her ivory silk suit was sophisticated, yet the cut was loose and casual enough to be comfortable. The orchid lei that her mother thoughtfully special-ordered in San Francisco set off a jade green silk blouse. Carved jade and ivory earrings added a touch of elegance against her thick blonde hair. Green leather sandals insured comfort. Only the unhealthy sallowness of her face from too many sleepless nights that refused to be hidden by makeup diminished the picture of natural elegance. She and the driver made their way to the baggage station and waited with the rest. It seemed to take forever.

To the carefree vacationer the changes were at first imperceptible—clusters of officials in serious, hushed conversation, additional policemen, a level of tense excitement that did finally cause a prickly uneasiness throughout the crowds of people. A sense of anxious curiosity grew; travelers unable to ignore the signs of impending trouble, but unwilling to believe that whatever it might be could invade their excitement. Instead, there was a good deal of tense laughter and hollow jokes masking real concern.

The loud speaker squawked and shrilled an announcement that was barely understandable, but the message sobered the crowd. "Incoming passengers who are staying in Waikiki area are advised that the entire area has been cordoned off due to a bomb threat. We apologize for the inconvenience. You will not be able to check into your rooms until the police have investigated and are confident there is no danger. Please stay in the airport and you will be notified when it is possible to proceed to your hotel. Those staying in other parts of the Island may proceed there, but you will not be allowed to drive through the streets of Waikiki. Mahalo—thank you."

"Thank goodness it's not going to slow us down. We can get to Kahala by another route, can't we?" Susan hoped her driver's answer wouldn't disappoint her. She didn't have the stamina to endure any last minute glitches.

The driver sensed Susan's fatigue. "Sure, Miss Michaels. We'll be fine. I'll just avoid Waikiki. You'll be there in no time, as soon as we get your luggage. Tell me what your bags look like. I'll get them, if you'd like to sit there in the coffee bar."

Bomb threat! Allison felt a stab of panic. What could she do? She had reservations at the Hilton in Waikiki. What if they didn't solve this before night? Going off by herself was a stupid idea, just like Joe had said. *Wait a minute, Al.* Allison mentally took herself by the shoulders, ordering herself to calm down. *Ninety percent of the people here are in the same boat. Somebody will come up with emergency plans. And you won't die if you have to sleep here in the airport one night.* She looked around quickly to locate a comfortable place to sit—this could take a while—and noticed a small coffee shop near the baggage area. It looked perfect, and she wouldn't have to drag her luggage all over the airport. Now if only her bags would appear.

Suddenly Allison thought of Glynnis. She must be panicked. Sure enough, when she looked over, her new companion had turned away, shoulders heaving as she cried.

"Look, Glynnis, this is not the end of the world. I know it's scary. Hey, I'm scared, too. This is a little more adventure than I'd looked forward to. But we'll survive. You'll see." Allison tried to make her words as lighthearted as she could. More lighthearted than she felt.

"This is just what I feared. I should never have come. I simply don't know how to deal with anything new or unplanned, and nothing could be worse than this! Bomb scare! My reservations are for the Ilikai. I understand that it is right in Waikiki. Now what can I do, sleep in the street like a vagrant? Allison, I'm trapped and I'm terrified."

Allison added several levels of calmness to her voice. She'd learned from soothing hysterical young ones what a quiet voice could do. "Listen, Glyn—do you mind if I call you Glyn?" Her friend nodded dumbly, not caring. "I promise you, we're in this together. I will not leave your side. If we have to find another place to stay tonight, we'll do it together. Just don't cry anymore on that lei. It cost money, y'know, and you're going to make brown spots on it!"

In spite of her terror, Glynnis couldn't help but smile. "In all my life I have never needed a friend more. Thank you so much. You can't imagine how deeply I appreciate your help."

"Hey, it's no more than I was taught to do in Girl Scouts, lo, those many years ago. Helping strangers in need goes along with assisting old ladies across the street. I'll bet you've done your share of that kind of thing, too."

The suitcases were tumbling down to the carousel and each of the girls soon claimed hers. Now they must figure out what to do.

"Just over there is a little coffee shop." Allison pointed to the right. "Let's hurry in before the crowd beats us to it. We can find a comfortable place to sit while this, er—complication—sorts itself out." She headed quickly to the door of the cafe and Glynnis followed as if a magnet kept her tightly partnered with her new friend.

Although they hurried, they weren't quick enough, for the tables had already filled with temporarily homeless travelers. Allison looked around the room and noticed a woman sitting by herself. Her body language sent an unmistakable message: 'I want to be alone.' *Nothing lost in asking, though,* Allie thought as she moved in the direction of Susan Michaels.

"I'm terribly sorry, but we're in a bit of a jam, as you must be. My friend and I are pretty tired and it looks like this bomb thing may take some time. Would you mind if we sat at your table, or are you expecting someone else?"

Susan yearned to say yes, she minded, that she just wanted privacy. But how could she? This was an emergency and she had to extend herself. "Of course, sit down. I'm alone. Actually I'm not going to be here very long, anyway. I'm one of the lucky ones that is not staying in Waikiki, so as soon as the driver picks up my bags, I'll be leaving. I hope it's not a long wait for you." Susan scanned the baggage area for her driver, wishing she could exit right now and avoid the inevitable introductions and small talk that would follow, but he was nowhere in sight.

"Thanks so much. My name is Allison and this is Glynnis. We are both visiting Hawaii for the first time, and it's a little unnerving to be hit with the bomb scare news. But it will be fine, I'm sure."

Emotional pressure was challenging Glynnis' will, and hearing the words 'bomb scare' again, and meeting this beautiful woman who was apparently immune to the problem set her crying. "I'm sorry. I just can't help it. I don't know what I'm doing here."

Susan was uncomfortable and prayed again that the driver would appear. She didn't know how to deal with tears or someone's inability to cope. Among Susan's colleagues there were no tears, and you looked out for yourself, fixed your own problems. Allison put her arm around Glynnis and said something quietly which quelled the tears. Susan thanked heaven that the histrionics were over, at least.

Just then the loud speaker screamed again. Everyone fell silent.

"Ladies and gentlemen, we're sorry, but the information we have from the Hawaii Police Department is that there has been a small bomb discovered in a Waikiki shop. It was defused and removed with no damage or injury to anyone. However, HPD must now make a thorough examination of the entire area to insure there are no more bombs and that the area is safe. That will not be finished tonight, I'm afraid. Visitors already checked into Waikiki hotels are being evacuated to nearby schools and auditoriums, and we are looking for more locations where you will be transported to spend the night. Please bear with us, as the number of people we have to accommodate is large and the available space is nearly exhausted. Feel free to use the airport benches to rest while you wait for further instructions. Again, we must offer our sincere apologies for the inconvenience. Mahalo—thank you."

Allison didn't miss a beat. She put her arm around Glynnis' shoulder and smiled, but found herself talking a little faster than she meant to. She hoped her less-than-calm attitude didn't betray her. "You know, Glyn, this reminds me of the years I was away at college. So often, going home for the holidays, I'd be on stand-by, hoping to get a seat at the last minute, and most of the time it worked. But I've cozied up on many an airport bench with a good magazine or book and slept until I could get a flight out. It was kind of fun—exciting—to be stranded and not know when you'd be able to go home. Didn't you do the same?"

"I went to Bryn Mawr, just a short distance from the my parents' home. I lived with them, so I didn't have to commute back and forth." Glynnis looked around nervously. "But none of that is important. I can't imagine staying in this airport all night! This is such a remote place—it's just not possible. Allison, can't we think of something else?" Her eyes were pleading.

Susan sat listening and watching, quite fascinated by the curious alliance between these two strangers. They could only have just met; they were about as far apart in personality and outlook as any two people could be, and apparently had no reason to seek each other out, yet here they were struggling to hammer together a friendship. Obviously one was helping, one being helped, but Susan sensed each needed the other right now. She admired Allison for taking charge when the woman must have been a little unnerved, herself, at this bizarre situation.

What startled her was that she began to feel an uncharacteristic warmness toward Glynnis. Susan had never wasted much time trying to pull anyone up by their bootstraps. In the dog-eat-dog world she lived in, you looked out for yourself, and her respect went to those who forged their way alone. But that was precisely the lifestyle that had sent her fleeing to Hawaii, trying to escape and heal, and she looked at this girl with a compassion quite unfamiliar to her. How was she so different from Glynnis? This awkward woman didn't seem able to cope with the real world unless chaperoned by someone, but what about Stalwart Susan? She had so channeled her energies into one realm—success in her career—that she'd painted herself into a corner. There didn't seem to be anywhere else to go. So what was so commendable about all this strength and drive? At least everyone could see that Glynnis needed help. But the world could only assume that Susan was sitting in the catbird seat. Little did they know. She shifted uneasily in her seat. Self-criticism wasn't her strong suit. Her attention shifted back to the conversation between the other two.

"Wish we had more options, Glynnis, but there's only two other choices I can think of," Allison carefully assessed their situation as she spoke. "Things will be in a mess all over this island, I'm sure. So our chances of finding rooms anywhere else are probably impossible. But we could try to fly to another island. Or, we could just turn tail and run home. What do you think?"

"Right now turning tail, as you put it, is an extremely inviting option. I hated the idea of this trip in the first place. Now I admit, I was beginning to feel committed to being here, even a little excited about seeing the Island. Since I met you, that is. But with this violence—a <u>bomb</u>, for goodness sake— being back in my own home where I'm comfortable and safe sounds marvelous. It wouldn't really be running away. We'd only be doing what any intelligent person should do, don't you agree?" Glynnis' eyes searched Allison's face, longing to hear her words of agreement with the idea of retreat.

"Hey, Glynnis, I don't blame you, and if that's what you'd rather do, let's get over to the airline counter and see if we can fix you up. They should be pretty understanding." Allison realized she'd already decided what her own plans were. "For myself, though, I really planned on this trip. Needed it. And I think I'll stick around here at the airport to see if things straighten themselves out."

Susan wished the two could be happily on their way to Waikiki at this very moment, like so many millions of visitors in normal times. "I'm terribly sorry your vacations haven't started out better for you. Glynnis, I don't blame you for being jittery with all this. But I'm sorry you'll miss seeing how beautiful Hawaii is—and how friendly. And Allison, with luck things will be all right by tomorrow and you can begin your vacation the way it should be."

It struck Susan that she didn't want to see these women disappointed in their plans. One of her talents as a trial lawyer was the ability to size people up, "reading" them, as she assessed clients and witnesses. And it was obvious that each of the two were struggling with personal issues, just as she was. Uncharacteristically, she wanted to lend a hand, turn their bad luck around. It would only be a day, she was sure. She cleared her throat and tried to sound natural, although this was definitely breaking new ground.

"Look, I'm staying at my parents' condo in Kahala. That's over by Diamond Head. There is plenty of room and all the facilities to be very comfortable. Why don't you both be my guests tonight, and tomorrow you can get over to your hotel rooms when they clear up this mess."

Glynnis gasped with relief, and Allison couldn't believe that she had just been offered a solution. She'd been prepared to sleep on the airport floor all night.

"I can't even go through the pretense of saying it's too much of an imposition on you. We're so thankful for your offer, and I think I can speak for both of us. We accept. I hope it's not too inconvenient. But you've really offered help when we needed it." Allison felt the knots easing out of her stomach, and heard a great sigh from Glynnis. She figured her friend would make it after all. For a while she'd had her doubts.

"Well, my driver's signaling that he has my bags, and I see you both have yours, so let's go. By the way, my name is Susan.

Susan Michaels. You both look pretty tired, but don't worry. We'll be at the condo in half an hour or so, and you can relax. I've come to these Islands since I was little, and never once left without feeling great. Of course, I've never been welcomed here by bombs and police, either. But if there's going to be an emergency, you couldn't be in a better place. Tomorrow you'll forget the whole ugly incident, I assure you, as soon as you get into the warm Pacific Ocean and feel the sun on your skin." Susan realized she was talking to herself as much as to the other two women.

## Chapter Two
# Later Sunday

**Eric Rogers proved** his skill as driver for the Palisades condominium complex during the next hour. Born and raised in Honolulu, he knew each back street and shortcut, and he needed every trick he'd learned to get Susan and her friends to the condo that afternoon. Traffic in town was always heavy. The combination of different cultural driving traits, throngs of office workers hurrying home, and countless tourists guaranteed a daily commute headache. But today was remarkable. All of Waikiki had been poured into surrounding thoroughfares, and so many were tourists who not only didn't know their way around, but were frantic because of this bomb.

Eric constantly marveled at how protected vacationers felt. People who doubtless fastened their seatbelts every time they drove, looked both ways before crossing streets, and in general took care of themselves and their children in a mature fashion back home became cocooned with a sense of immortality in Hawaii. They were on vacation. What could happen to them in this Heaven? Talking animatedly to one another, they'd step off a curb and into the street without a single thought about traffic. Abracadabra—safe. But today their bubble of protection had burst. Fear and uncertainty made them edgy. Suddenly the island was small and they were vulnerable. There was no safe and familiar place they could go. It seemed all they could do was mill around in circles, waiting for someone to yell, 'Cut!' to end what was too much like a scene from a bad movie.

Artfully Eric laced the big car away from the crowds of tourists, the going-home commuters that gridlocked every intersection, and the myriad of buses trying to move displaced hotel occupants to safe havens. Although not a typical tour of the city for first-time visitors, his route gave Allison and Glynnis glimpses of the Honolulu of many years ago—older homes festooned with orange and crimson bougainvillea, lanais looking out onto narrow streets that hadn't changed much in thirty years. Garden jungles offered the fragrances and colors of multitudes of gardenias, hibiscus, orchids, white and red ginger, clustered amongst banana, plumeria, Chinese Banyan, and palm trees. Somewhere a ukulele strummed lovely Island melodies. Hibachis and barbeques proclaimed with tantalizing smoky whiffs that the grilled dinner of choice on the island was teriyaki.

Eventually they reached the Kahala district and Eric pulled up to the plush condo.

"I'm sorry it had to be such a difficult trip home, Miss Michaels. I know you and your guests are worn out. Go on in and I'll follow with the baggage. Noelani will have some cold drinks ready, I'll bet." He opened the car doors for the weary travelers.

Susan opened the door to the condo and turned to guide the two girls in, but noticed they had lagged behind, standing in the middle of the driveway gazing out at the view. She smiled wistfully, wondering how it must feel to experience this for the first time.

"Remarkable, isn't it?" Her companions nodded silently as

they pulled themselves away from the view of Diamond Head and the sparkling ocean framed by palms to follow Susan inside.

Allison and Glynnis were overwhelmed by the apartment. It was mostly windows, each one looking out on a perfect scene—some toward the ocean and Diamond Head, others toward the lush mountains, the rest offering views of exquisite gardens. Just as Allison noticed at the airport, even though they were inside the house, it was simply an extension of the outdoors. Openwork wooden panels, beautifully carved in Oriental designs, allowed the trade winds to flow through the rooms and also set a stunningly elegant mood. Polished marble floors added to the overall beauty and coolness. Rattan furniture upholstered with subdued ice blue and emerald green leaf print material offered comfort as well as esthetic perfection. There were countless bouquets of fresh flowers, artistically arranged.

"Susan, this is spectacular. You must come here all the time. It's so breathtaking, how can you ever leave?" Allison didn't mind letting her amazement show.

Susan had to admit that she'd ignored the place. "It's probably impossible to believe this, but I've been so busy these last years, I guess I just haven't been here for a while. It sounds strange, but somehow work took over, and I haven't had time." Her voice trailed off. She was shocked at how embarrassing it was to confess her addiction to her career. Until this minute it had not occurred to her that she was cheating herself of this relaxing pleasure and enjoyment. Work was her pleasure, her life. It was challenge she enjoyed. Now she cringed to think how that must sound to her two guests, and realized she was apologizing to herself, as well. Startled to uncover such a vulnerable spot, Susan quickly changed the subject.

"Eric was right, we could all use some refreshments. Let's see if the housekeeper is as on-the-ball as he claims." She darted out of the room and into the kitchen area to gather her composure and to call Central Housekeeping.

"I feel sorry for anyone who can't take time out to enjoy a place like this." Allison's feelings were heartfelt. "Most of us have to work hard, but if you can't enjoy yourself from time to time, what's the sense of it?"

Glynnis found it strange that their self-assured hostess had chinks in a personality that before had seemed enviably flawless. "She is so beautiful and composed. It surprises me that her life is not picture perfect. But she sounded a little melancholy when she spoke about not being here recently."

"Looks like there are three of us who are lucky to be vacationing right now. You're fortunate to be here, too, you know, Glynnis, whether you think so or not. Those dark lines of worry on your face when you got off the plane have disappeared! Well, almost, anyhow."

"I don't believe you, but thank you for bolstering my courage. And it is true, I almost forgot myself as we were driving here, and looking out at the sea from this place. How perfect it is. I never expected such beauty." Glynnis made a small attempt at enthusiasm and found it wasn't as painful as she'd expected.

"Noelani will be up with some drinks in just a minute. I took the liberty of ordering a pitcher of Mai Tais and one of iced tea." Susan had regained her equilibrium and seemed in control again as she came back and sat down.

Allison glanced at her watch and realized she needed to

contact family and assure them she'd arrived safely, and to explain where she was and why.

"Do you mind if I make some phone calls, Susan? I promised I'd call as soon as I got settled, and people will worry if they don't hear from me soon. If they've had any reports about this bomb thing, they'll be frantic."

Susan showed her into a bedroom where she could make calls in private. It was strange calling back home to Joe. With all the commotion and excitement the last little while, Allison had been able to separate herself from the nagging worries about their relationship. Alaska, and her life there, seemed planets away. She called and was saddened that there was none of the old ease that had always been so normal between them. The conversation was friendly, but stilted.

Joe hadn't had the T.V. or radio on, and was unaware of the emergency Allison had faced. "Christ, you'd better just turn around and come home. That's no place for you to be alone."

Allison assured him she'd be fine, and that she would stick to her plan, even though he made it clear he didn't approve. He was uneasy that she had gone in the first place, and jumped at anything that would end her trip. "You and our kids belong here, at home, instead of farming them out to your folks and racing off on some cockamamie jaunt," he had lectured her before she left. When Allison argued that since he refused to talk meaningfully with her she needed to get away to sort things out, Joe refused to respond. He seemed to have lost control of events, a situation unfamiliar and uncomfortable to him. Even so, he did nothing to alleviate the rift, so she had to do something on her own and for herself.

It surprised Allison that the conversation left her feeling

more self-assured as Joe sounded quite lost at sea. She smiled as she visualized him as she knew he'd be—sitting at the dining room table, feet twisted around the chair legs like a little boy, with the phone propped characteristically on his shoulder. "I love you, Joe. I worry about you, too, you know. So be careful and take care of yourself."

"I will, Sonny. I love you. And I miss the heck out of you." Allison was startled to hear words of tenderness, the first in weeks, and felt pangs of sadness when she heard his familiar nickname. To her friends she'd always been Allie, but Joe created his own nickname from the last part of her name, so it would be his alone. "I hate to see an important part of someone's name just discarded and neglected like that," he'd joked. But it had always touched her that he had wanted a private connection with her.

Fighting back the emotions that crowded up in her throat as she put down the receiver, Allison dialed her parent's home in Seattle. One part of this trip that had worked out well was that her folks had pleaded for months to let the children spend time with them, and this was the perfect opportunity. The two youngsters had leaped and shouted with glee when they were told they'd be staying with Grandma and Grampa for two weeks. Their grandparents made life wonderful when they visited, taking them to all kinds of special places and knowing just what kids loved.

Allie's mother, Marilyn, answered the phone, and was relieved to hear her daughter was alive and well. "We thought you might have been taken hostage by a bunch of terrorists or something!" The nervous strain was apparent in Marilyn's voice, though she tried to joke with her daughter.

Allison explained she was perfectly all right, even though her hotel arrangements were in limbo. She described pairing up with Glynnis, the chance meeting with Susan and how she had taken them in. As soon as she was confident her mother had relaxed about her safety she demanded a full accounting of how the kids were, what they had been doing, how they were behaving, and all the motherly concerns that came into her head.

"You've been giving Jill the medication for her ear infection every day? Are you making sure Bobby does his share of the chores?" Of course, Allison knew she had nothing to worry about. Her mom was the model of organization, never letting anything slip her mind or neglecting any responsibility.

Marilyn explained that the children were out with their granddad. "They left early this morning for Pike Street Market to watch the fresh fish being unloaded, and then were out discovering most of the day. After dinner here they all decided to go to a Walt Disney movie. You know your dad. He's as much a kid as they are. He goes off with them every chance he can."

It was hard to end the conversation without talking to the children, but Allison made arrangements to call the next morning, quickly hung up, and joined the others in the living room.

"Allison, I envy you having people who care so much about where you are and how you are. I'm an only child, and my parents both died recently. Even when they were alive, I never really went far enough away for them to wonder how I was. They were in delicate health for many years, you know, and I took care of them." She paused. "Didn't do much else." Glynnis sounded wistful. "Of course, I must call Uncle John." Another hesitation. "He's not really my uncle, but my godfather. An old family friend I've known since I was a child. John was Father's lifelong friend and his lawyer, and when Father died just weeks after Mother passed away, he convinced me that I should come on this trip to get away and relax. A couple of hours ago I was furious with him for pushing me into it, actually demanding that I go. But now I think he knew what he was doing. I'm going to call him and tell him he's not the ogre I thought he was!"

Allison laughed to see how relaxed her new friend had become, and Susan found it remarkable that the tense bag of nerves she'd met at the airport had unwound just a bit. Glynnis disappeared into the bedroom to call John.

"Glynnis, is that you?" John Halverson's voice was shaky with sleep. "Are you all right, dear? I've been worried half out of my mind, thinking I'd sent you off to a terrible fate."

"I'm perfectly all right, Uncle John. Now that I hear your voice I know I awakened you. I had forgotten about the five-hour time difference. I'm so sorry."

"Never you mind, my dear. Just tell me if you're all right." He was beginning to wake up despite the fact his bedside clock confirmed it was after midnight.

"Oh, quite fine, John. I'm still a little shaky about being here, especially since we seem to be under siege by a mad bomber or some such disgusting thing. But a very nice lady I met at the airport invited me to stay with her until tomorrow, when I'm sure I'll be able to get to my hotel. And don't worry, John, she is a very responsible, trustworthy person. Truly a Good Samaritan! You know I wouldn't go off with just anybody." She hesitated. "I do admit, on second thought, that I should have been more skeptical about doing this, but I was so thankful to have a place to go when we were told we couldn't get to the hotel, I jumped at the invitation." Glynnis was startled to realize that this was the first thought she'd given to her safety when she agreed to go off with Susan, a total stranger. Never in her life had she acted so impulsively or irresponsibly. But she controlled her panic, telling herself there had been circumstances that excused such unusual behavior. She gave John the telephone number and quickly finished the conversation so he could return to bed.

Glynnis stepped back into the living room to find that the housekeeper had, indeed, brought refreshments. Two trays were placed on the coffee tables in the center of the room. One held the icy pitchers of tea and drinks, the other an array of sandwiches and an irresistible bowl of fresh tropical fruits.

The women hadn't realized how very hungry they were. It had been hours since they'd eaten, and the excitement had drained their physical as well as emotional reserves. Their last meal had been lunch on the plane, which seemed eons ago, and they eagerly attacked the food.

Noelani returned to tell Susan that friends of her parents had invited her to spend the evening with them. Susan was perplexed, undecided about what to do. She felt a little uncomfortable having two guests unexpectedly. In a way it would be nice to slip away and visit with family friends. But she had assumed a kind of responsibility for them, even found herself warming to the two girls, and hesitated to leave them on their first night.

Allison jumped right in. "Susan, don't think about the two of us. We'll be fine here, and after such a long day, we will both head for bed soon. You go ahead." Glynnis nodded in agreement.

"That's nice of you, Allison. I don't know. I'm tired, too. I think I'll just stay here tonight. Noelani, would you mind calling the Comptons. Please thank them, but tell them I'm exhausted from the trip. I'll call them in the next few days and we can get together." Susan felt better knowing she could just stay home and relax, and she expected the other girls would go on to bed soon, as they planned. Entertaining them would be too much tonight.

"Let me show you your rooms so whenever you want to turn in, you'll know where to go." Susan tried not to make this sound like a veiled suggestion that they retire now. "Eric said he put your bags there already, so you're all set any time you decide to call it a day."

"One thing I'd like to do before turning in is to catch the news. We need to find out if we have any hope of getting to Waikiki tomorrow. Since you got us out of the airport and into this heavenly place, it's hard to imagine that we could be tossing and turning on a hard airport bench right now." Allison wondered as she spoke how this was going to play out. Were they going to be able to resume their vacations tomorrow? If not, she'd probably have to consider turning around and going home. There'd be no other accommodations available, she was certain of that. *Think about that tomorrow, Scarlett*, she reminded herself.

Susan turned on the TV and the girls settled into big arm-chairs watching with fascination to see what fate held in store for them. For the first time in several hours, Glynnis became fidgety and couldn't seem to get comfortable. Reality struck a warning note in her head once again.

The news could have been worse, but certainly was not what they wanted to hear. After an exhaustive search, no more explosive devices had been found, and a man had been arrested. Seemingly, the suspect had been stalking his ex-girlfriend, who was a cashier in the small Waikiki boutique where the bomb was discovered. The day before the incident the store employee had demanded that the man stop harassing her, informing him she would call the police if he continued. He became enraged, yelling threats which were overheard by several salespeople and customers.

It appeared that the case was a closed matter, but as the police investigated the suspect's past they found a history which made them cautious. He was an unsavory character with a police record. And he told the police he had hidden two more timed devices in the area, but wouldn't cooperate and tell them where.

The authorities had already conducted a search throughout Waikiki and were confident the area was clear, but they could not reopen it to normal business until they were sure beyond a doubt that it was, indeed, safe. Although they would not confirm when hotel guests could check in, they conceded it would not be until late the next afternoon, at best.

"I don't know how they'll be able to know for sure that it's safe, no matter how carefully they check it out." Glynnis hadn't completely forgotten the idea of bolting and running.

"Don't you worry, Glyn," Allison spoke firmly and reassuringly, looking directly into her eyes. "Nobody's going to go off half-cocked. Look how careful they're being. They say they're sure right now it's okay, but they're going to take extra measures to check again. They've got very sophisticated methods of locating bombs, you know. I don't feel nervous at all. And by tomorrow night we'll be settled into our own hotels."

"I wish I had as much strength as you do, Allison. I worry too much, I realize that." Glynnis slumped a little in her chair as she mentally castigated herself for her weakness.

Susan spoke with a protective tone in her voice. "No one in their right mind would criticize you for worrying about this, Glynnis. You're doing great. But Allison is right, things will be safe again, don't worry."

"I have a great idea," Allison broke in excitedly. "Why don't you plan to share a hotel room with me, Glyn!" I don't relish the idea of going solo on this vacation. We could have a ball, don't you agree? I'd really love to pair up. It's so much more fun to do things with someone else. Come on, Glynnis, let's do it! Anyway, I recall sort of promising you we'd stick together. Remember?"

Glynnis immediately brightened as she realized that she might actually enjoy her visit to Hawaii now that things had taken such a fortunate turn. "You know, it might really be fun, Allison. We could tour the island and see the sights. We could swim at the beach and go shopping for tourist things." She hesitated for a moment, wondering if she was allowing her emotions to do the thinking when she should be more careful.

Smiling broadly, she added, "And I know Uncle John would be relieved to know I won't be alone. It's the prudent thing to do, isn't it! Do you know something? Prudent or not, I'd love to do that. This could turn out to be a wonderful vacation after all!"

Susan was listening with surprise to this change of pace. She felt like getting just a little involved in the planning, too. "I think I could help make it more fun, if you'd like a tour guide now and then. I'm a little rusty on what's going on here, but

I'll bet I could take you to some pretty nice spots. Some of the 'must-see' places, and some that are hidden treasures. Be sure and get in touch after you've moved to the hotel, and we'll spend some time together, if you want."

"Hey, this afternoon I wouldn't have bet too much on these two weeks, but here we are ready to turn in tonight in the loveliest of places, with tomorrow looking great, and everything turning out swell. And Susan, your suggestion is perfect. If you can stand being branded a 'tourist' with us in tow, we'd love to see more of you. Come on! You're the heroine of our Survivors' Club." Allison stood up, hugged Glynnis and Susan and smiled. "We three are going to have some fun!"

Glynnis stifled a yawn. "But right now, we should get some sleep. I'm suddenly exhausted. Anybody else?"

"You're talking to the Zombie Patrol. I'm on my way to bed, too. What a day!" Arms stretched straight ahead of her in sleepwalker fashion, Allison marched toward the hall.

Feeling awkwardly motherly, Susan sent them off to bed with a final pep talk. "Hope everyone sleeps well tonight. I'm sure we're all dead tired, so that shouldn't be a problem. Ring the intercom to my room if you're in need of anything. Sleep in as long as you'd like, but you don't want to miss too much of the first real day of your vacations. I'll begin my tour guide duties as early as you want."

"Sayonara, everyone. I can't wait until tomorrow, Susan." So saying, Allison led the way down the hall to their bedrooms.

## Chapter Three
# Monday

**Glynnis slowly opened** her eyes the next morning and bolted upright in bed, unable to remember where she was. She began to panic, but then remembered yesterday's events and gradually pieced together how she came to be in this lovely room. Looking around her warm, yellow and white bedroom, she noticed the sunlight caused everything to glow. Despite familiar rumblings of misgiving, the serenity and luxurious comfort of the place enveloped her in a blanket of safety, and she relaxed.

*This is beautiful beyond imagination. It's like finding myself on a movie set. Every detail is perfect, so magical.*

Then her thoughts turned into a familiar and timeworn trail. *But my decision to stay here is insane. I've fallen in with total strangers! I must be the most gullible person in the world right now. I've let yesterday's emergency and the beauty of the Islands lull me into a terribly compromising position. I don't even know these people, and there's no excuse for me to be here. What am I thinking of! Did I ask to see anyone's identification? No! It's not too late to extract myself and get home, though. That's what I'll do, this very morning. I'll just change my return reservations and get back where I belong, no matter how embarrassing. I don't care how breathtaking this is.*

Glynnis turned wistfully to look out the window one more time. The room faced into a small Japanese garden bordered by a slatted fence. Her breath caught as she tried to absorb the beauty, so different from anything she had ever seen before.

The garden had been landscaped by an artist, simple, but perfect in its beauty. Volcanic rocks surrounded a sparkling pond which was shaded by Egyptian papyrus and bamboo. Floating lily pads provided hiding places for several fat koi that swam lazily, their golden, black and ivory hues appearing as shifting shadows, gems tossed into the cool water. A stone lantern stood in the center of a small sea of sand, carefully raked in a way that reminded Glynnis of ocean currents. There were Bird of Paradise plants, hibiscus in a rainbow of colors, gardenias, and lovely flowering shrubs that she couldn't identify, all creating a wonderfully quiet retreat. Slipping through the sliding doors, Glynnis stepped out into this idyllic spot, breathing in the fragrances carried on the breeze, awed by the beauty.

She crossed the pond on rustic wooden planks that led to a small bench. Sitting there, looking across the garden to the mountains—the Koolaus, she remembered—Glynnis struggled with very new and uncomfortable feelings.

*Go back home to what? All my life I've been too afraid to do anything that wasn't prim and correct, living in the shadow of Mother and Father, quite happy to throw away my life in return for their protection. How easy for me. I didn't have to make any decisions. Father told me how to manage my affairs, Mother steered the rest of my life. And I patted myself on the back, thinking I was the perfect daughter, noble because I remained home to ease their lives. Yesterday taught me just how pathetic it is to be a mature woman running like a scared schoolchild whenever there's trouble, waiting for someone else to solve my problems, and whimpering like a baby all the while. There's not much nobility there.*

*And I don't have one friend to call my own. They're all from Mother and Father's social circle. Certainly good people, but there's not one of them that I chose as a friend. I just inherited them, like everything else. My whole life is second-hand!" Glynnis cupped her forehead in her hands, despair flooding her soul.*

But slowly she straightened and shifted decisively on the bench. *But I DO have friends. Allison and Susan! Well, a few hours together don't really cement a friendship, but it's the first time I've established a relationship with anyone on my own. It's a start. I'm not going to run home with my tail between my legs. I'm going to stick it out here. No, not stick it out. I'm going to enjoy this vacation. I won't be my own worst enemy any more. In less than a day I've seen more beauty, experienced more drama, and felt more kindness directed right at me than ever in my whole life. I'm living my own life! The next two weeks are going to be different. No more being terrified, afraid of my own shadow, like an ostrich with my head in the sand. I'm going to do this. I <u>can</u> do it, and I will!*

Glynnis gazed beyond the garden at the mountains, so strikingly green. They looked ancient, mysterious, and underlined the fact that she was, indeed, very far from home. Wispy clouds hung in the deep valleys and sun struck the timeless promontories, creating a ballet of light and shadow. She recalled her father reading tales to her of warrior kings and strong queens, great battles and the warm, friendly Island people, and was again astonished to be here, experiencing this for herself.

*At least I'll have one spectacular memory for my old age,* she murmured. *One that's mine alone.* With that she breathed deeply, re-entered her bedroom and dressed for the morning.

"But I must get some other shoes!" she laughed out loud.

Allison was awake, but refused to open her eyes for several

long minutes. Instead, she lay quietly, listening to the sounds of the Islands—pounding surf, rustling palm fronds, birds celebrating the morning with their songs in the garden. Yesterday's lei hung next to her bed and its sweet perfume filled her head, almost too much pleasure for her senses. Tending a rambunctious family in rural Alaska didn't yield many self-indulgent moments such as this.

*I've found heaven,* she thought happily. *and I don't ever want to leave.* Allison jumped out of bed, her impatient nature refusing to miss another minute of the morning. After a shower that completed the waking up process, she chose a thick-piled towel from a stack of crimson and orange, perfectly matched to the cascades of bougainvillea outside the bathroom window. *Whoa, this is something. I wonder if Susan realizes what bathroom towels look like when you have two kids,* she laughed, remembering the tattered collection in her linen closet. *A proud statement of familyhood,* she thought, content with her well-used assortment. *But hey, I can handle new and luscious—I could get used to this quite easily. But I'm not ready to trade in the kids for anything in the world—yet. They'd better be careful and behave like angels, though, or out they go!* Allison enveloped herself in the soft towel and scrubbed herself dry, in that moment entirely happy with her world.

She suddenly paused. *What in the world am I doing? This is crazy. Here I am, so content with life, quite relaxed and enjoying this glorious place. How can I be so goddam happy when my whole life is collapsing like a house of cards. Everyone always praises me for being in control all the time. Hah! What good is that if it just means I've always compromised on everything in the name of a happy marriage, and now look at it! It's not that I'm so in control, it's just that I'm a jerk.* She pounded her fist into the perfect towel. *We had a terrific, loving relationship. We shared so much together, worked as a team, and cared beyond words about each other and the kids. But now, I just don't understand why it's happened, but he's changed. All of a sudden his personal life is strictly his business. He snaps at me if I ask ordinary questions about his activities. 'I'm not a child, I don't need another mother.' I can't believe he'd say that to me simply because I wanted to know if he'd be home in time for dinner. Let's face it, whether he'll admit it or not, he's got somebody else.*

She shook her head slowly from side to side, trying to organize the thoughts that continued building. *But since this Other Woman thing happened, it's forced me to look more carefully into our whole relationship. I can't back away from the fact that he doesn't really value me. I'm part of a package, and a pretty much taken-for-granted one, at that. I come installed with whatever it takes to provide him with tidy house, great children, hot meals, clean clothes. Also perpetually ready to hunt, fish, can, preserve the wealth of Alaska to sustain the family. Just like in the novels. 'While she juggles perfect wifeliness in the air with one hand, she can be counted on to grab the chainsaw or the axe with the other. She will shovel snow, clear brush, scare moose out of the vegetables, defy bears.' That's with the third hand, I suppose. 'And in case you didn't notice, folks, she never complains. She is supremely happy, has no gripes. And look at her, my friends. She loves to wear old Levi's, heavy woolen jackets, stupid looking fisherman's hats, layers of gloves, sweaters, socks, boots—good 'ole Ma Kettle. And to keep the romantic flame alive she gets all gussied up, puts on perfume, lathers hand cream on cracked hands. Voila! A new woman. Not tired because she's worked all day and tended sick kids. No, never! Just the greatest, sexiest thing this side of Las Vegas.' Oh sure, but that's not enough! He doesn't even notice anymore. It's much easier, and I suppose very exciting, to just start fresh. Well, good luck, Joe!*

Allison was now taking it out on her hair, scrubbing it furiously with the towel. She enjoyed this fuming, getting satisfaction from letting it all out. The more outraged she became, the more punishment she dealt her scalp.

*I'm going straight home to tell Joe I've had it. Who does he think he is? He doesn't know how lucky he is, and maybe it's just too late for him to realize it and change.* She tightened her jaw in defiance and scowled.

In mid-scowl she remembered what her kids told her: 'Mom, we always know when you're really mad, because you tighten your jaw that way. It's a dead giveaway. Even when company's around, you might talk nice to us, but when we look at you, we know we've had it, and we're going to hear about it later!'

A wide smile broke out that changed her whole face—and relaxed her jaw, as well. She began stroking her hair thoughtfully and with care, a reprieve from the beating it had been taking.

*Okay, things are turned inside out right now, but I'm a grown-up girl. I can figure this out. That's what I came here for, right? I'm still on course. I just don't know what the heck the answer is, but then, I've got two weeks to get to that. Don't know if I can do it, but it's worth the effort. Stick to your plan, Allison. Don't back down now, just because you frightened yourself with your own tight jaw trick!*

After fixing her hair and pulling on new shorts and sleeveless top she'd bought for the trip, she headed for the living room to see how the others had fared overnight.

Susan's eyes opened, but she lay perfectly still, not knowing how long she'd been awake. For the first time in weeks she had known restful sleep, thanks to the balmy air, tropical sounds and a work-free schedule, fueled by exhaustion. It was a good feeling, and she couldn't help stealing some extra time to luxuriate in the pure comfort of it. But in a corner of her mind that had not totally slowed to low gear, something kept working. Events of the past months were running through like movie stills. Susan didn't know exactly why, and didn't care.

*I don't need to remind myself of all that's been going on. That's what I want to forget for a while,* she told herself. But the reruns kept rolling.

Susan tried to change direction and think about what she could do to entertain her guests. They deserved a great first day, since their vacation had started off so poorly. There were many choices, but she wanted to pick the best one to launch them into the kind of holiday they deserved. Then they would be off on their own, of course, in Waikiki. And she could rest.

*They'll be settling into their hotels some time this afternoon, I'm sure, so I'd better plan a trip that won't take too much time. Maybe a nice drive to a beach for a picnic—somewhere they can swim and get some sun.*

First memories of Hawaii crowded in, and she saw herself as a tiny girl stepping out into the warm water, laughing and splashing with her dad. "Peanut, you're a fish! With that bright pink swimsuit of yours, you look right at home in there with the other tropical fish. Remember all those Hawaiian names I read to you? You laughed when I said 'Humu humu nuku nuku apua'a,' but it's a real fish name! Now, what shall we call you? I know, you're the Haoli fish, the 'Outsider.' After you've come here with us for a few years, we'll change it to Kama'aina fish—someone whose heart belongs here because they love it so much!" Susan smiled at the thought of that first swim and her dad's loving words. She'd been just a toddler.

*A toddler. Imagine. What a lot of fun I had in those days. I was no more than a baby when I learned to swim . . .*

She bolted upright in bed. Something hammered in her brain, but she couldn't get to it. And she was surprised at this walk down memory lane. Definitely not like her.

*I'm just tired, no doubt about it. One good night of sleep isn't going to cure that, I guess. I just need some time, that's all it is. Laying out in the sun on warm sand today will be a great way to relax. By the end of the day I'll be more like my old self.* And, she quickly remembered, she'd have the place all to herself, so there wouldn't be a constant pressure to entertain her guests. *Tonight I will sit with a book and read just for the pure joy of entertaining myself and relaxing. Not one legal issue to probe. What a luxury. And Allison and Glynnis will be fine, happy to be on their own, I'm sure. I'll just drive to their hotel to see them a couple of times and show them around. That will leave me with time to rest up and get myself together.* She dressed for the day, reassured, and stepped out into the living room to check on her guests.

Glynnis sat alone in the living room and watched the morning T.V. news with great interest, fascinated that her life was dramatically entangled in the major news story. And the news was good. Developments early that morning led authorities to estimate they'd have Waikiki cleared for use by early afternoon. Details of the police investigation satisfied even Glynnis there was no danger. Just as the news ended, Susan came down the hall into the room, and Glynnis smiled warmly as she passed on the information.

"It looks like we'll be able to leave you in peace this afternoon, Susan! The police say that Waikiki is safe and we will be able to get to our hotel. Hotel guests who were evacuated yesterday will be allowed to return first, then it's our turn to check into our hotels. Then you'll have your privacy again."

"Well, I'm very happy for you. Of course, it's been no imposition at all having you here." Susan was quick to assure her that the unexpected stay had been just fine. "But I know you're anxious to really get started on this vacation, and where better to be but Waikiki—the heart of Aloha!"

"Oh, yes, and now that Allison and I have decided to share quarters, I'm very excited about it. I'm going to miss this place, and you, though. No hotel could match the companionship and beauty here."

As they talked, Allison popped her head around the corner of the room and waved cheerily to her friends.

"Aloha, girls. We're still in the land of palm trees and gentle trade winds. Can you believe it?"

The other two smiled as Allison added her special bright touch to the morning.

"I don't know about you two, but I'm starving." Susan realized they'd only had a light dinner the previous night, which would explain why her stomach was tugging. "We can go out somewhere, or I can ask Noelani to bring breakfast here from the main kitchen. I'm voting for 'Lani's great food, because Mother has told me she's a culinary artist—and it will take much less time!"

"Don't have to convince me. Let's order here." Allison looked at Glynnis. "What do you say, Glyn?"

"You two speak for me, too. Could we eat out in the garden? It's so beautiful this morning."

"Of course, a perfect idea. What would you both like?" Susan looked from one to the other.

"You're the expert here, Susan. Why don't you decide for us." Allison looked toward Glynnis, who nodded in agreement.

Half an hour later breakfast arrived, a colorful plate of papaya with lime wedges, scrambled eggs, Portuguese sausages and toast. A large carafe of steaming Kona coffee completed the meal. As they relished their meal, they were charmed by the colorful birds that darted around them in the trees, some intrepid enough to approach the table and snatch bits of food that had fallen to the ground. They laughed at the bold ones, the Mynas, Bulbuls and Brazilian Cardinals with their striking red crest. Susan tried to name the many birds that flew into the garden while they watched, explaining that some, like the Java Rice Birds with their thick pink beaks and dumpling-round white cheeks, were escaped cage birds that found the climate to their liking and flourished. They laughed at the flock of shy Japanese White-eyes as they skittered through the branches, so tiny and almost weightless that they could hang on the smallest bough.

The women ate with enthusiasm and chatted happily about the day ahead, agreeing with Susan that a visit to the beach would be perfect before checking into their hotel in the afternoon.

"Let the pageant begin!" Glynnis felt unusually gay and adventurous, then immediately foolish, as she toasted the plan with her cup of delicious coffee. The day promised excitement and a level of happy anticipation she was not accustomed to.

"I think you're going to like the beach I've chosen. At least I hope so. It's not a tourist spot—you'll get a lot of that in Waikiki. This is a place I've gone for years, and I love it. Lanikai, which means beautiful beach. We'll drive over to the Windward side of the island. Life is quieter there, it's the real Hawaii. The beach is—well, you'll see. Susan arranged with Noelani for a picnic lunch and ordered a car for the day. Within a half-hour they were ready and set off. The drive along the coastline to the eastern side of the island kept Allison and Glynnis in a state of amazement, pointing at beautiful vistas around every turn and chatting with excited animation.

"Now, this is what we came for! Look at that bay down there! I've never seen such blue water. It's like a jewel." Allison stretched her head out of the window to get a glimpse of this most lovely cove.

"That's Hanauma Bay. We'll go there, but let's save that for a day when there's more time. I won't even begin to explain Hanauma to you. You'll have to see for yourselves. Complete with snorkels!" Susan's words intrigued the girls, who could hardly wait to do just that.

Soon they drove into the town of Kailua, and Susan explained that many people who worked in Honolulu commuted across the island in order to live in this beautiful spot. "They drive over the Pali Highway every day."

"Lucky people. That's the road that goes over those striking mountains, isn't it?" Glynnis looked up again at the lush green spires that pulled at her emotions so strongly. "And I believe there's a lookout at the top on the spot where King Kamehameha tossed his enemies over the cliffs to their death when he conquered Oahu." She shivered.

"You're right about the Pali, Glynnis," said Susan, "but drivers don't really feel all that lucky to tackle it every day. It's a bear of a commute. Half of the island is trying to get to the same place from here, and it's hectic. Sort of like a cattle run. Let's face it, even though the view is spectacular, commute traffic is never fun. I must say, however, if you have to drive to work, this is infinitely better than the miles and miles of concrete and billboards that most people deal with daily. Besides, as bad as it is, I don't think I've ever found more congenial drivers than here. They communicate with one another through hand motions—'I just need to cut in here so I can turn right, won't you let me in?' one will signal, and the other driver will let them in! Yes, they're polite, although it makes for some crazy traffic patterns." Both visitors smiled and agreed the commuter here shouldn't complain too much.

They ambled through the small town, noticing the pace was much like any small town on the mainland. No bright lights, no motel or neon signs. Just people going about their daily affairs. Turning into the residential district, they marveled at the gardens, overflowing with rich blooms bestowed by the tropical climate.

"What a way to live!" Allison was amazed at the contrast with her own home state. "I love Alaska, and I'll always want to live there. But when my ship comes in, I think I'll buy a summer place here—maybe that one!" She gazed at a home that was quite simple, but roomy, and boasted a wide lanai that looked out over a green lawn framed in coconut palms. "I guess seeing those children playing so happily has something to do with my choice!"

"You must miss your children, Allison. I don't have any

of my own, of course, but if I did, I know it would be hard to be away from them." But just remember, you're only here on vacation. Before you know it, the two weeks will be over, you'll be going back to your family, and you'll wonder whatever happened to the time." Susan's voice was wistful. "You're a lucky lady."

Allison sobered as she realized that in a few days her vacation would end and that would bring a return to her world—and problems. She would make decisions in the coming days that would affect the rest of her life. It seemed so bizarre. But there was no denying it was happening. She shook herself out of her musing, not wanting to throw a wet towel on the day for the others. *I'll work it out,* Allison told herself.

"This is Kailua Beach Park, a wonderful place, itself. They do a lot of windsurfing here. In fact, Robbie Naish, one of the first windsurf stars, came from Kailua. We're going just around the corner up there, to Lanikai. It's really an extension of Kailua in a way. No stores, just homes. And the beach." Susan smiled as she heard the exclamations of approval from the others.

The road led them into Lanikai, looping up against the side hill and then around to the homes on the ocean side. Susan found a parking spot next to an access trail leading to the beach.

"Let's get the lunch hamper and towels and find a spot, ladies." Susan started down the trail, surrendering herself to the warm breezes and sound of the surf. "Now we can all start to relax!"

The day was perfect, full of swimming, playing in the surf, sunbathing. The sand was clean and white, sparkling in the sun.

All around them the brilliant greens of the palm trees and tropical vines were framed by a sky too blue to be real. And when they ran like young children into the ocean, the soothing warm water cradled them gently as each girl basked in her own reverie. After a swim they were ravenous, and devoured their lunch of sandwiches and fruit, laughing and joking all the while.

"I don't know where the time has gone, but if we're going to check into our hotel we'd better think about leaving, don't you think, Susan? " Glynnis didn't want to leave, but it was important to make their hotel arrangements before it got too late. "If we don't hurry, they may give our room to someone else." Worry lines started across her forehead.

"Oh, Glyn, don't fret." Allison laughed. "I secured the room with a credit card. It's all paid for, so there can't be any confusion." *There could be, though*, she told herself, *with all the craziness that's been going on these two days*. "But you're right, Glynnis, we should probably get settled in. I sure hate to leave this place. Can we come back, Susan? I think I could come here every day of our vacation."

"I know what you mean. I told you it was one of my favorite places. This is about as perfect as a place can be. There's a lot more to see, however. So be ready to be overwhelmed. Better pack up and get into town. We need to stop by the condo and get your things, and I will bet the traffic in Waikiki is going to be a disaster."

The drive back to Kahala went quickly, filled with happy chatter about the success of the day so far and questions about what to expect at the hotel and in Waikiki. Once at the condo, they hurriedly packed the few things they'd taken out of their bags, and Susan called the driver to take them into town. As Eric once again exhibited his talent at navigating through traffic jams and steering them to their destination without incident, Allison and Glynnis felt thrilled to be in the heart of Waikiki at last, and gaped in wonder and without shame at the happy chaos that enveloped them. The car turned into the entryway of the Hilton Hawaiian Village and they admired the brilliant mosaic tile rainbows that decorated the buildings. It was as though yesterday's frightening incident had never happened.

Suddenly Allison realized their first adventure was going to end here. The unwritten episode of bomb threats, unexpected delays, a new friend and good Samaritan was over, and the original phase finally about to begin. She'd expected it would be a happier occasion, but she hated to see Susan drive away. She could tell Glynnis felt the same, noticing her friend was quiet and had turned away, not wanting to make eye contact. But Allison wanted Susan to appreciate how much her efforts had helped them and to see nothing else. Her face brightened and she smiled broadly.

"I wonder how long it's going to take us to be out on that beach. Got to get on with this constant pleasure, right Glynnis? Susan, come on in if you'd like. I know you've probably put off so many engagements to show us around, but we'd love you to stay awhile if you can."

"I really have to go, Allison. You're sweet to invite me, and I will come back in a day or two to see how you both are doing. I'm just a little tired right now."

"In that case, thanks again for the helping hand. You saved our bacon! I won't forget it, Susan." Allison was teary-eyed as they hugged.

"Oh, Susan, I never thought I'd be this happy. I owe you so much. I just can't say good-bye. Please come right back over and see us tomorrow if you can." Glynnis squeezed Susan's hand.

"Of course I'll be back. How can I leave you two to fend for yourselves? I've enjoyed this time, too. So take care and give me a call tomorrow." It struck Susan that she was a little sad to see them go. Well, of course they were nice, and had been good company. But she'd had enough hostessing. She quickly smiled and jumped back in the car, not wanting to make this good-bye any harder for her friends. As Eric started the engine, she waved as her companions headed into the lobby.

The two women were quickly absorbed into waves of visitors milling in the lobby and as they waited at the desk to check in, their eyes darted from one luxurious detail to the next, caught up in the excitement of being in this dream world. Lighthearted madness ruled as hotel guests jostled each other, jubilant they could now move into their quarters without worry of explosions or evacuations. But Glynnis and Allison didn't notice the waiting at all, so busy were they with 'gawking,' as Glynnis called it. Eventually they were at the front of the line, and Allison was signing in for the room when she felt someone grab her elbow from behind.

"Don't do this. Come back with me. I don't know what I was thinking of, I really don't want you to leave now. It's not the same as staying here, of course, but I'll bring you down to Waikiki and we'll prowl the streets and buy tourist things and do all that. I really want you to come home." Small tears balancing on Susan's eyelids erased any doubt in Allison or Glynnis' mind that she was serious about her offer.

"I couldn't believe we were going to be separated so soon. You bet we accept." Allison knew she spoke for Glynnis, too.

After hurriedly canceling their hotel arrangements the threesome raced to the car and returned to their new home, confident there was no one happier in all the islands. The rest of the evening was spent unpacking, enjoying a festive dinner, and relaxing on the lanai, making plans for the following days. Then, tired and happy they set off to bed, anxious to get started tomorrow.

*Chapter Four*

# Tuesday

**She was a** tiny child in an amusement park, laughing and playing with her parents, when suddenly she became lost. Her mother and father were nowhere in sight and she saw only strangers who took no notice of her. She ran through winding paths, searching for that wonderful smiling face of her dad, but he had disappeared. Her eyes strained to find Mother's open arms, but no one reached out to her. Running this way and that she finally flung herself down, exhausted, on a bench and sobbed. She felt people looking at her, and couldn't understand why they wouldn't help. She was all alone and it was getting dark and she would never see her family again. It wasn't fair for a little child to be so abandoned! She was a good girl and didn't deserve this. How could Mother have left her there like that? With a sudden jolt Susan awoke and sat upright in her bed. She shook her head to rid herself of the traces of sleep and the dream, and sat wondering why on earth her mind had taken her on such a disturbing journey.

*I'm easily spooked these days. I don't know why a dream should upset me. Just when I need to lie in this bed for hours of wonderful, uninterrupted sleep, here I am playing the idiot, working overtime trying to find something to be upset about. Let's see, how would Mother dramatize it? Ah, something like, "The only thing worse than seeing one's world tumbling askew is realizing that one's own meddlesome fingers have done the skewing." She's a ham, to be sure, but you can always find the kernel of truth in her sayings.* Smiling, she straightened her covers, turned her pillow over to enjoy the coolness of the unused side, and tried to settle down. She was determined to drop off into a blissful sleep devoid of dreams. Through the open window she heard rustling palm leaves, the surf breaking in the distance, occasionally the noise of a passing car. Rather than dropping effortlessly into sleep, uneasy thoughts niggled at the corners of her mind, and she was helpless to make them go away.

Sitting up once again, trying to relax, she silently scolded herself for becoming so snarled in this stream of worry. As she took a deep breath and started to lie down for another try, her eyes opened wide and she steadied herself with both hands.

*My God, I'm pregnant! I know it. It's crazy, but that's it. No wonder I've been so out of control. No! I just can't be! It's just impossible. There is no way this can be happening.*

But slowly she thought about it, and realized it could, indeed, be happening. You were never completely protected. It must have happened that night during those hectic weeks when crisis was the order of the day at work and her relationship with Philip was in turmoil. Years of built up pressure had been working silently to erode her stamina, setting up a network of fissures that suddenly began exploding, splintering, as Susan envisioned her life tumbling into ruins, but could find no way to stop it. Even as she tried to work with Phil to find a compromise, to build on the love they had and not allow it to unravel, she saw herself bungling it. Every thought she expressed sounded hollow and weak, her viewpoint selfish and inconsiderate. She thought with bitter humor about the old adage that the lawyer who hires himself in his own defense is a fool. She was sinking, but couldn't find the strength to pull herself out of the darkness of defeat. Helpless and frustrated, she gave up.

They split up and Phil moved to a hotel. But because they were both unhappy with the loss of their relationship, he'd persuaded her to take time out to go to dinner a couple of times, hoping to work things out, and once, quite unexpectedly, what started as dinner lengthened out to include the night. They talked over breakfast coffee, desperate to find a solution, but Susan refused to change her decision to separate. The passion that had resurfaced couldn't erase the major difference in their expectations. Philip understood that Susan wanted to continue her work after they married, but he wanted a traditional marriage, including a family, at some point. Susan didn't have anything against children, but knew that motherhood wasn't for her. She had a strong determination to keep life uncluttered so she could pursue her work, and that wasn't compatible with motherhood. There could be no compromise and so they had come to an impasse, and painfully parted company.

*I know it happened. I know I'm pregnant. God! My head has been somewhere else these last weeks. I must have been walking around in a fog, missing the signs. Well, I'm going to have to do something about it immediately. At least I'm on vacation, away from home, and I can take care of it with no uproar. Thank heavens for that, anyway.*

Susan realized that she was already making plans without confirmation that she was pregnant. *I'll get a kit. I know what it will say. But I'll do it right away. Then I'll get in touch with a doctor.* She jumped out of bed, noticing the early hour, showered, dressed, slipped out of the quiet house. She found a twenty-four hour drugstore not far away, purchased the home test kit, and returned long before anyone else stirred.

Just after nine o'clock she came into to the living room, pale and drawn. She'd known the test would be positive, but even so, the reality of it was jarring. Her friends sat in the livingroom studying maps brought from the hotel lobby, and she heard their animated discussion. Susan regretted asking them to return, but suddenly she knew she had needed them here. Perhaps she'd realized at some deeper level what was happening and had reached out to these women to be with her. How strange. Not at all in character, but there it was. No need to tell them about it, of course. It would only disturb their holidays. Besides, she couldn't imagine allowing people to intrude that deeply into her privacy. Enough that they were there. She'd go ahead with her plans without saying anything. Might be a little difficult, but Susan knew she could pull it off.

"You know, kids, I've got a great idea for today, if you're game. Let's go into Waikiki so you can do all those tourist things I pulled you away from when I dragged you back here. There are a couple of errands I have to take care of, so if you don't mind, I'll drop you off and we can meet for lunch at one of the hotels. Then we'll spend the afternoon in the shops. To top off the day in style I will introduce you to a couple of the most outrageous tropical drinks at the Sheraton poolside bar. You'll have fun watching all the other tourists—and they'll probably be watching us! Sound like fun?" Far from the ordinary errands she alluded to, Susan had to contact a doctor and make arrangements for terminating this pregnancy. She tried to lighten her voice with gaiety, hoping it didn't sound as stilted and insincere to the girls as it did to her.

The day's plan did sound like fun, and soon Allison and Glynnis were poking their heads into small souvenir shops and crowded bazaars, excitedly trying on swimsuits, buying T-shirts and customized coffee mugs, laughing as they decided what to do next.

"I've never bought so many useless things in my life!" Glynnis giggled as she held up a T-shirt that proclaimed 'Life's a Beach.' "I could never wear this at home!"

"Good for you! While I, of course, have been my usual, practical self, buying only necessities. But I ask you, how many times do you think I'll wear my new flowered playsuit in Homer, Alaska? Can't you just see me out halibut fishing in 30 degree weather wearing this brilliant red hibiscus print?" Allison did an impersonation of herself hauling in a huge fish, teeth chattering, knees knocking from the cold, pretending to take one hand from her imaginary fishing pole to massage the opposite shoulder for warmth, causing them both to shriek with laughter.

The morning flew by and the women were startled to find it was time to meet Susan for lunch. They walked toward the hotel where they planned to meet, laughing about the flurry of things they'd seen and done. Of course they'd have to give Susan a full accounting, and laughed even more as they realized what a frivolous morning it had been.

The hotel restaurant was lavishly decorated in a nautical motif, and waiters wore swashbuckler outfits of tight black pants, full-sleeved white tunics and bright red sashes. Black bandannas knotted over one ear and eye patches guaranteed the effect. The maitre'd informed them they were the first of their party to arrive and pointed out a table near a replica of a pirate ship.

Glynnis was wide-eyed. "Susan said that Waikiki was the

best place in the world to people-watch, and I'm beginning to agree with her. There's so much going on, and visitors must come here from every nook and cranny of the world. I could sit here all day and do nothing but watch. Isn't this fun? I've never 'gawked' before!"

Glynnis' remarks caused Allison to smile, realizing how little of life her friend had experienced. "I know. But don't forget, just like Susan said, all those people we're watching are watching us! Probably saying the same things. Look at us, carrying eight or ten shopping bags, wearing shell leis, hats that say 'Aloha, Paradise' across the front, and showing the first signs of a sunburn. We literally shout TOURIST! But so what if we cause people to roll in the aisle, I don't care, do you? I'm having a ball."

Glynnis sobered. "I know I don't have to tell you, Allison, that I'm not accustomed to doing things like this. I never would have, either, if it hadn't been for you. How can I thank you enough?"

"For heaven's sake, Glyn. What did I do? We bumped into each other during a really weird time, and we decided to weather it out together." Allison caught sight of Susan approaching the table. "And in the process, we found Susan. We're an unlikely trio, but I think we have the makings of a great team."

"Well, here you are. I don't have to ask how the morning went. Look at you! How are you going to get all this stuff in your suitcases when you leave?" Susan was genuinely happy to see her friends, but she thought, *Please don't let them notice anything different in my attitude. There's nothing they need to know. Let me act relaxed and casual.* The appointment with Dr.

Liu had been routine, and he had given her instructions to consider her options carefully and return in a few days if she still chose abortion. Dr. Liu had stressed to her that this decision merited careful reflection and counseled her to discuss it with the baby's father, whose wishes should be weighed, also. The emotional impact of the appointment left Susan nervous and agitated. She prayed she could carry this off, but it didn't take long to realize it wasn't going to work.

"Susan, if I didn't know better I'd say you'd had some bad news. Have you been talking to your office or something?" Allison spoke with the same insight and concern she showed to her family. "You'd better sit right down and have something to eat. You're as pale as a ghost."

"It's nothing that a good lunch won't cure. I guess I just can't leave the worries of real life at home, that's all. Forget it, and let's order." So saying, Susan picked up the menu and described the many tempting dishes to the others.

"It's going to be something from the ocean, that's for sure, but which to choose? I don't have any idea. These names are nothing I've ever heard before. Maybe Hawaiian fish are a little too—bizarre for me. Perhaps I should order something else. I'm not an adventurous eater." Glynnis remembered her favorite Eastern fish entrees, but hesitated at these odd names. "Opakapaka? I don't think so."

"Trust me on this one, Glyn. Just order the Catch of the Day and you won't be disappointed, no matter what it is. I guarantee there's no need to be squeamish. Are you willing to gamble?" Susan smiled encouragingly.

"What are you going to order?" Glynnis looked nervously across the table at her partner.

Allison put down her menu, laughing. "We're not in Alaska, that's for sure. No king salmon or halibut here. I'm afraid it's the blind leading the blind, Glynny, except for our friend Susan here. So I'll go with that Catch of the Day. Let's see what they've hauled up for us."

Lunch was a success. Both visitors raved over their fish, delicately delicious and hinting of ginger, served on a banana leaf, while Susan chose a bowl of clear soup. "I'm saving up for tonight's meal," she argued when Allison questioned her.

After lunch, there was more browsing through the shops, and by late afternoon everyone agreed they wanted to call it quits. Susan escorted them to the pool bar she'd described, and they relaxed with the promised tropical drinks complete with plump spears of pineapple and tiny, colorful parasols decorating the glass. Susan explained when Allison noticed she hadn't ordered for herself, "I've had enough of those elaborate concoctions in my lifetime to know better! Besides, it's more fun watching you two."

"My new sandals are comfortable, but six hours of pavement is enough. I could stand to get home." Glynnis showed signs of fatigue. "I'm going to the Ladies' Room to freshen up, if anyone else would like to go."

"Thanks, I'll be fine. You go along, Glyn." Allison waved cheerily as Glynnis headed around the deck lounges and into the hall. Then she turned to Susan, glad to have a moment to speak alone. "Susan, you've got a right to your privacy, and I'm not one to intrude. But I sense something's not right and if you feel like discussing it, I'm here. Just know that, okay?"

"You're kind, Allison, and I appreciate your thoughtfulness—and your intuition. But I'm okay. Maybe later we can talk." Allison respected her friend's wishes and changed the subject. They chatted about the days ahead and what they might do. Susan relaxed a little, although Allison worried about her drawn face.

Suddenly Glynnis reappeared. She tried to look calm, but knocked her chair out of place as she sat down and apologized with a shaky voice to the guest seated behind her.

"My heavens, Glyn! Whatever has happened to you? You were just gone a minute or so and here you are looking like there's been another bomb discovered in the women's bathroom." Allison didn't know whether to laugh or not, seeing the other woman so agitated.

"Oh, nothing. Really. Well, in truth I had a rather unpleasant experience, but it's all over now." She clutched her purse and sat down. "Susan, do you remember I told you I always feel uncomfortable getting up in a public place and walking past all the guests to get to the restroom? I said it feels like everyone is looking at me, knowing where I'm going, and that embarrasses me. You gave me a tip. You explained your imaging technique, picturing yourself confident, purposeful, comfortable and in control of the situation. You said I should imagine that people were looking at me in admiration, not laughing at me.

"Well, I tried it just now, and even though I was a little nervous, it worked. I thought of myself as Grace Kelly. She's my favorite actress. So regal, and a Pennsylvania girl, just as I am. Do you remember her in 'High Society'?" Glynnis unconsciously straightened in her chair, lifted her chin a little and smiled serenely. For a second she was lost in her memory of the lovely Grace, perhaps dancing effortlessly across a marble floor, the crystal chandelier overhead casting sparkling reflections on the diamond tiara settled in her thick blond hair. She shook herself and quickly returned to the reality of where she was, and continued the story. "Unfortunately, I was focusing so intently on my conception of myself, I must not have been paying enough attention to what was going on around me because suddenly a scruffy, unshaven man nudged against my shoulder and grabbed at my purse. But, thanks to you, instead of panicking and becoming paralyzed with fear, I thought of a movie I'd seen where the actress handled a similar situation, and I copied her. I guess it worked because the pickpocket jumped back into the crowd and disappeared without even trying to take my purse. Well, then I sort of lost the imaging technique and more or less came unstrung, but when I saw you girls, I knew I'd made it! I'd handled the situation, and pretty well, too, if I do say so myself."

"Glynnis! You can't mean it! You poor thing. What did you do that frightened him away?" Susan put her arm around her friend's shoulder.

"Well, in the movie scene the girl was accosted by a terrible rapist, but she had taken lessons in self-defense and knew just what to do. She yelled some aggressive, threatening things in a very loud voice to startle her attacker. I just did the same thing, and it worked."

"You're terrific, Glyn. And brave!" Allison beamed at her friend with both surprise and admiration. "Whatever did you say that sent him running? These guys can be pretty rough."

As she spoke, Glynnis felt her cheeks turning a flaming red. Her voice wavered. "I just sort of said what the actress said: 'Keep your hands off my purse, or I'll kick you in the god-damned testicles. It seemed to do the trick, all right!"

"You said THAT?" Susan felt her mouth drop wide open in amazement.

"Yes. Just like the actress in the movie. Well, she didn't say exactly—that. I couldn't remember the word she used, but that's what she meant."

Allison's eyes met Susan's. Without saying a word to embarrass their friend, they shared a feeling of immense shock. Glynnis had said—no, she hadn't *said* it, she'd screamed it out in front of a whole crowd! Totally unbelievable. Allison wanted to laugh, but knew she must not. While forcing herself to use gutter language to defend herself, Glynnis had done it in the most socially acceptable, dignified way she could. But save herself she had, and Allie knew this was a monumental step on the road to self-confidence.

"You've really got the right stuff, Glyn. Good for you!" Allison smiled warmly at the embarrassed Glynnis.

"I can't thank you both enough for giving me a little courage to be my own person. I'll never forget how much you've helped me. I know I must be a bit of a drag, but if it's worth anything, you've both done something for me I never thought would happen. You've helped me stand on my own two feet." Glynnis looked from Susan to Allison with admiration and gratitude.

"You're not the only one, Glyn. What it is I can't quite understand, but you know, the three of us are good together. Some unusual chemical mix that just works. You could say the sum of our friendship is greater than the individual parts— synergism." Heads nodded in agreement with Susan's assessment of the fledgling coalition. "We haven't known each other for very long, so you really have no way of comparing, but my normal role is pretty much that of the lone wolf. I pride myself on being self-sufficient and—well, I guess unapproachable, if I'm honest. It's not that I dislike people, quite the contrary. Glynnis, you just now used the imaging thing to pull yourself through a difficult situation. It's a terrific technique. I've used it throughout my career It's sometimes pretty tough sledding to be a woman in the legal field. I'm not complaining. I think I've achieved what I worked for without dealing with too many obstacles along the way. But to develop strength, I used those very strategies I explained to you to remain totally self-contained, earning everything I ever attained without asking anyone for help. Only now I wonder if I should look for a little different direction. I think I've built some pretty thick walls around a one-dimensional box and it looks like I've maybe locked myself inside. All these years I've called it self-discipline and focus. Now I wonder if I wasn't just clinging too tightly to the one thing I could do well because I was afraid to tackle the rest of life. I don't know. These are pretty confusing times for me.

She shook her head. "But I'm probably boring you to death, girls! You spent your money to vacation, not to be eyewitness to a talk show tearjerker!" Susan tried to regain her composure, surprised at her revelations. *I am in a weakened state,* she thought to herself.

Allison hesitated for a moment. "I don't know about you guys, but I could use a little time to let down my hair, too. To tell the truth, my life is not in the best shape right now. Sue, you're worried that maybe you haven't stretched enough. With me, it's kind of the opposite. I've stretched out to cover all the bases, taking care of everybody. But I've noticed recently that I'm out there alone in left field, unprotected. Like when somebody keeps pulling the blankets over to their side of the bed until your rear end is out in the cold." She paused, frowning, then smiled. "And you're the one who knit that darned blanket in the first place! No, I wouldn't mind letting a little synergy go to work for me!"

"Oh, heavens. I thought I was the only one with problems. You two seem to have such perfect lives, while the whole world has been able to watch me flounder and flail around from the time I set foot in the airplane." Glynnis looked sheepishly at her friends. "But oh, please don't misunderstand. I don't mean I'm happy you're troubled. That's not it. Not at all. I am sorry if there are things worrying both of you. It's just that somehow it makes me feel a little more—more normal, I guess you'd say. Is there anything I can do for either of you to help? I'm not very good at this, but I'd like to do something."

"Thanks, Glynnis. We'll all be fine, I'm sure. We'll work out what's worrying us. I sure hope so, anyway!" An uncharacteristic tiredness sounded in Allison's voice as she answered.

"Let's call it a day and get on home. We can have a light dinner and then talk the night away if you want." Susan was fearful about discussing her condition with the girls, but somehow it felt right to do just that. She wished she were convinced that this was a right move—she was still a little dubious. Susan lectured herself, *Lady, I hope this limb you're climbing out onto doesn't come crashing down.* But she turned to the girls. "So what do you say?"

"Only if you have dill pickles and peanut butter at home, Susan." Allison noticed a touch of tension and attempted to alleviate any misgivings. "In high school my best girlfriend and I had many a 'nightover' together. We'd talk into the wee hours of the morning about teachers, homework, our favorite music, and especially boys! And along about midnight we'd sneak out into the kitchen and fix toast, spread it with peanut butter, top it with a slice of dill pickle and put it under the broiler. It's heavenly. Soothes your soul, I promise. Everybody ready?"

*Chapter Five*
# Tuesday Evening

**Settling in back** home, the three friends enjoyed a light dinner on the front terrace. Nearby in a massive old Chinese Banyan tree, what sounded like thousands of mynah birds chattered as they found roosting places for the night in the branches. The women were exhilarated by the tropical aura that surrounded them.

"Who needs windchimes when you have that many birds singing," Allison laughed. "Isn't it beautiful, though?"

They relaxed quietly as darkness robbed them of the glorious view, then walked back into the house, sorry to say goodbye to the day, a little apprehensive about the evening to come. The day's conversations had led them to agree to disclose protected parts of themselves, peel back a layer, share secrets, and each wondered if it had been foolhardy to let down their guard so easily.

Susan adjusted the lighting in the living room to a soft, low glow and rummaged through the collection of CDs to select music. She found her favorite Hawaiian music, slack-key guitar artists—Gabby Pahinui, Ozzie Kotani, Leonard Kwan and Sonny Chillingworth. Her father had explained to her that when the guitar was introduced to the Islands through its cowboys, called paniolos, local musicians adapted the instrument to their musical style by "slacking" the strings, tuning them to different keys. The result was rich and inventive, and became the sound of Hawaii. Music floated softly through the room, and for a few moments the three sat silently, carried away by the fluid sounds.

But soon the mood changed imperceptibly. They shifted uncomfortably in their seats. Susan hoped someone would begin talking about their day of sightseeing, something they'd noticed in Waikiki—anything to steer the conversation back to the earlier nonchalant chatter. But curse it, she had opened this door, for whatever inane reason. She had only herself to blame if strangers entered her private world. She hadn't felt close enough to any women to share personal problems for so long. Since high school. Maybe it would feel better to get it out in the open. A big 'maybe.'

"I swear, this is like going out on a first date for heaven's sake! I'm all nerves!" Naturally it was Allison who found a way to break the tension. "If I remember correctly all we agreed to was to be good friends and let down our hair a little. And only if we want to. Let's just talk. And I promise you, I don't have any ugly, dark secrets to divulge. I'm not wanted by the Alaska State Troopers or anything! In fact, I'll go first." Despite the banter and her typical light attitude, it was hard for Allison to speak frankly, difficult to sort things out clearly enough to define her problems. Her voice became more serious, tentative, despite an attempt to keep it breezy.

"You're about to hear the true life story of one Allison Kathleen Bradley. In a nutshell. Let's see. Grew up pretty normally, a typical American kid. Great parents, wonderful hometown, good friends. Got pretty good grades all through school, loved sports. And after college, got married." She grew more quiet. "I've had what my friends describe as the

perfect marriage. Joe and I love each other. We have a marvelous family, a small, successful business in an awesome
place. We were college juniors when we met and it was the
old storybook 'Love at First Sight.' On graduation night Joe
proposed to me. He came from Alaska, I was born in Seattle.
We settled in Homer, Alaska, started the flying service, and I
think we've done well with our plans, fulfilling our dreams.
Until recently I was happy, my life felt comfortable, so simple and right. It's difficult to believe how everything changed
in such a short time.

"It happened suddenly. Joe went to Anchorage for several
days. There were some airplane parts he wanted to look at, a
little insurance business to go over with our agent, and as long
as he was in town, he decided to get his annual physical.

"When he got home I asked how things had gone and he
barked at me that I shouldn't be so nosy. I tried to jolly him out
of his funk, but he got up and went outside without a word.
Slammed the door. That's not Joe. He started snapping at me
every time I said anything, I chalked it up to overwork or money worries. Then I noticed that when I started a conversation
about the kids or the business, he'd mumble something that
showed he wasn't listening and wander off. *Don't push him too
hard, lighten up,* I told myself. So I made more private time for
us and tried to fan the romantic flames, get his mind off his
troubles. Let me tell you, if you've ever had someone turn
their back on you in bed when you thought you were being
your most romantic, it's a sure sign you're not succeeding, and
definitely a downer!"

Allison shrugged and smiled, took a deep breath and continued. "Well, after a lot of frustration and hurt I drew the

only conclusion I could. Joe was tired of me. He'd fallen out of love. I tried to live with that, but it's not my way to just accept something that devastating. I'm a fixer. So we talked. That is, I talked. Joe sat there, but he wasn't even listening, let alone talking. The status quo apparently suited him just fine. I think he hoped if he just ignored me for a little longer I'd finally get tired, just drop it and get used to our new relationship. I couldn't believe he wanted that or expected I could live with it. Then something happened that stunned me, but it explained everything.

"One afternoon there was a phone call for Joe from someone named Rachel. 'Who's Rachel?' I asked with my best Raggedy Ann look—big, innocent eyes, benign, goofy smile. His answer was short, but it told me all I needed to know. 'She's an old high school friend, and please tell me why I have to justify to you who I see or talk to?'

"Well, folks, it ain't hard to add up the obvious. He's in the middle of an affair. With 'Rachel.' Whoever that is. Some 'Rachel' who doesn't know me, who's never seen our home, doesn't know our kids, has never worked for one day to make our business succeed. A 'Rachel' who apparently can walk in during the second act and take over my husband and my life.

"Naturally he won't confirm it to me, but he doesn't deny it either." Her voice had quieted and she seemed to be slowing to a stop, but she rallied a little. "So here I am holding the bag, so to speak. It's my move—time to fish or cut bait. I figured if I got completely away from him and the kids I could get a better grasp on what's happening and on myself. Have time to think. Hope it works."

The room was quiet for long, painful minutes.

"You've been so ready to help me, Allison. How could you have kept cheerful and interested in what bothered me, when you're the one with real problems. You seem so—so relaxed! I just want you and your husband to be happy again." Glynnis put her hand on Allie's arm, patting her affectionately.

"Oh, things will work out for the best. Don't you worry, Glyn. At least I don't have a bear clawing at my back door!" Allison's attempt at humor sounded thin and unconvincing.

"Well, you both know my story." Glynnis plunged bravely in to move the attention away from her friend's sadness. "Everyone knows my story. I told you I've never had the courage to do anything for myself. Mother and Father protected me. Mother was terrified of any activities that took me away from her side, away from her protection. As I grew up, I wasn't allowed to go on school field trips or to parties, not even to the houses of school friends. She fretted that I wouldn't be adequately supervised. Father didn't seem to worry as much about those things, but he was concerned about shielding Mother from anxiety, relieving her fears, so he agreed. After a while I felt different from my schoolmates, and I'm sure they felt the same about me. Eventually it didn't even occur to me that I should have a life outside my own home.

"I don't blame my parents for my life. I should have stood on my own two feet. I should have been thinking! But I succumbed to the idea that it was my family duty to stay close to home, and because of that I fled from any challenge to be my own person. Now I see that it was easy for me to close my eyes. By sacrificing independence, I never had to take any chances, risk anything. It was safe. Safe and dreary.

"If I chose colors to represent the three of us, I'd choose sunflower yellow for you, Allison—warm and cheery. Susan, I think of purple—royal, composed, dignified. I'm a very dull, unrelenting gray.

"You've both seen to it that this is going to be the vacation of a lifetime for me. But I still know I'll be going back home soon, and it will be the same as it's been all my life. Except now my parents are gone. I won't be able to kid myself about the real reason for being a scared rabbit. I'm just a spinster and all alone, and all that will change over the years is that I'll become an old spinster. But believe it or not, that's not the way I want it to be. I wish I could change my life. Too late, I think." She wiped her eyes and looked glumly at the floor.

"Shame on you for giving up on yourself, Glynnis Paxton! If you just lie back and let yourself fail, you'll have only your-self to blame. We haven't known each other very long, but al-ready I feel close to you. I want you to be happy, just as you told me. Don't let me down now!" There was warmth and a solid determination in Allison's voice. "You can do it, believe me! And don't forget, you've got us as a new support system. We're here for you!"

Susan thought how safe it would feel to find herself in a courtroom instead of here. Trial work was her life, her first love. She was comfortable there, on familiar ground. It was home, where her talents shone through, and friends and col-leagues recognized her accomplishments. It was second na-ture to listen to stories like those of her houseguests, to look at their situations, and then to analyze their needs, assess their strong points and weaknesses, weigh options for them to consider. Advising someone else was what she did every day. Plunging headlong into a disclosure of her personal life and troubles to others was an unheard of invasion of her privacy and unbalanced her dignity.

Reflecting, she wondered if perhaps it was not so much an unwanted invasion as a luxury she had never allowed herself. Wouldn't it be comforting to let someone else care about her worries and pain? And wouldn't it help? She'd watched Allison and Glynnis get to know each other, feel so easy together. And it was plain that each genuinely cared what happened to the other. What did she have to lose if she confided in these two friends? *It's pretty easy to see I don't know where I'm going with the decisions I've got to make. Surely I can't lose anything by showing my hand to them.*

Ever since leaving Dr. Liu's office, her initial simple decision to terminate this pregnancy and get on with life had been in total disarray. He hadn't advised her against it or suggested what she should do, but he had gently opened her eyes to how dramatic her course of action was. She was astonished to realize she had made an instant decision without weighing the facts or the consequences, and had not considered anyone but herself. Especially Philip. This was his child—a child he wanted. Didn't she owe it to him to discuss it together? It appalled her she had been so blinded by self-interest. And what did she owe to this baby? God, when did she become so selfish?

Susan cleared her throat and spoke uncertainly. "Back at the hotel bar when you described your pickle and peanut butter midnight special, Allison, I suspected you'd read into my mind. It seemed you already knew I might be leaning toward yearnings for bizarre food. Could be I am, because nothing ever sounded so tempting!"

Allison was startled. "Susan, I really didn't know. You're pregnant, aren't you! How could I have missed the signs? You haven't eaten properly for days, no alcohol or coffee, and you've been so dragged out. Guess it was easy to just blame it on the overwork you mentioned. Are you all right? Is it okay?" She studied Susan's face for a reflection of her mood.

Glynnis jumped up and hugged Susan. "Oh, I feel like I'm going to be an aunt! I know that's silly, but I do. I'm so happy." She paused awkwardly. "Dear me, Susan, I forgot that you're not married. You may not be as excited about this as I am. I'm acting foolish again, aren't I?"

With difficulty, Susan proceeded. "Well, Glynnis, it's complicated. I have a career that consumes my life, and I love it. There hasn't been much time for anything else. Except Philip. Philip and I really hit the right note together. We enjoy the same things, respect each other. Whether we're debating some issue for hours on end or sitting quietly together reading, we're comfortable. We love—loved each other, and made plans to be married. I laughingly said it would be a marriage made in heaven because he loves to cook and I can't unwrap a loaf of bread. Then he brought up the subject of having a family, and I was honest with him. I said I couldn't imagine having a child. Not only was there no time for it, I didn't think I'd be a great mother. Not a good idea.

"Philip explained that he most definitely wanted children. It didn't have to happen immediately, and it didn't have to interfere with my career, but there had to be a family in our future as far as he was concerned. We spent some tormented weeks trying to work it out. I wasn't in good emotional shape anyway, but even so, there's no compromising on something like that. We split up, the marriage plan dissolved, died. That was when I fell apart at work and took time off to come here.

Allison and Glynnis sat silent as she continued. "When I discovered I was pregnant, there was no doubt in my mind what I should do. I saw a doctor in town today to discuss an abortion." Glynnis drew in her breath and Allison stared at the floor, understanding Susan's quandary, suffering with her, voicing no opinion.

"You're not going to keep the baby?" Allison's question was gentle, quiet.

"I wasn't going to, didn't even consider keeping it. But after seeing the doctor I realize I can't make that kind of choice without a lot more soul searching. It's not just my life I'm dealing with. I recognize that now. But how do I find the answer, know the right thing to do? I'm used to taking control of situations. Now I feel as helpless as a child."

"Don't worry, Susan. I have watched you these last few days. I know you're a good, caring person, and intelligent. You'll work it out. You will. And we're here to help if you need us." Glynnis reacted with an uncharacteristic command of the situation. "Don't you worry, we're all in this together. But you look tired. A good night's sleep is in order right now."

All heads nodded in agreement. Glynnis knew this dramatic evening shouldn't go on any longer, and her suggestion to call it a night brought a sigh of relief from the other two. After some small talk Allison hugged Susan and Glynnis and set off for her room. Glynnis followed, and Susan began the nightly routine of closing up the house. She was about to turn off the last light when she decided to fix a cup of tea and sit alone awhile. She brushed aside the remembered admonition repeated by her mother so often as she grew up: 'Any dilemma envisioned in the dark teems with ogres, demons and gargoyles. By morning's light, the monsters disappear, being only gloomy shadows of the night.'

*Mother can be pretty eloquent at times,* Susan smiled at her mental image of the warm and intelligent woman with a dramatic flare tempered by a good measure of humor. *Maybe that's where I learned how to talk to a jury. I wonder how she'd deal with this doozy. Certainly she would wait until morning, but there's no time to lose, and my only other choice is to toss and turn for hours. She does advocate a warm cup of tea to calm you when you can't sleep, so at least I'm batting five hundred!*

Susan picked up a pencil and legal pad, guided by the habits of her profession. She intended to commit to writing all the issues involved, possible solutions, concerns. To move a problem from your head to paper gave you the power to deal with it, analyze, solve it. Her pages of notes for any case were like worry beads. Relentlessly reading and rereading them defined the real issues, and once uncovered, she could tackle and bring it all to a satisfactory conclusion. There was one significant distinction, however. Tonight the dilemma was about herself, about the rest of her life. Perhaps the most important issue she would ever deal with. The pencil hovered over the pad of paper and, receiving no instructions, refused to do anything but make swirls on the pad, loop following loop, aimlessly biding time. Her mind wandered dreamily, and the pen dropped to the desk while thoughts played through her head flowing from an obscure hiding place in the brain where old memories lay dusty and dormant.

There could be no better place to grow up than the pine

forests and white sand dunes of Carmel, California. There was beauty and mystery, and legendary ghosts populated the beaches and hills. Daddy loved his "Peanut" beyond measure, and Mother laughed and played with her, almost a child herself. Young Susan instinctively knew there had been a baby before her, but something had happened. No one discussed the details, yet she knew the love flowing to her had been meant for two. Even as a tot she romanticized the details of a lost sister or brother. Thoughts of a little child fading away from a mysterious illness or a band of kidnappers swooping down on an unsuspecting young one filled her imagination with mystery and romantic notions. But, too, the knowledge of her parents' loss placed a responsibility on Susan. Although glorying in the pampering, and cherishing the happy attention, she tried always to respond with true devotion and not self-centered egotism, repaying such love with a happy, generous and warm spirit.

From her Father came a love of adventure, the desire to discover new places and learn about whatever caught her attention. Together the two would walk the beach, searching tidepools to study the briny inhabitants. Long walks in the woods provided ample opportunities to study the plants, trees, birds and animals that they encountered. During times together the scope of their conversations was endless. Both enjoyed sharing opinions. Susan listened, the student learning everything she could from her beloved father's comments. Paul Michaels was equally delighted with what she had to say, fascinated to watch the process of learning and logical thinking unfolding in his precious daughter.

Mother brought high drama and magic into Susan's world.

Herself a thwarted actress, Peggy Michaels had long ago stopped pining over her lost chance on the stage. She'd described to her daughter the realization that she wasn't really in love with being an actress, she simply loved the theater, as she did art and literature. Mother had read to Susan for as long as she could remember, fashioning a wonderland of rich feeling that encompassed the tragic, passionate, comic, poetic, whimsical. It was she who related the many tales of Carmel's early days, cementing Susan's love of the place in its colorful artistic history. She created images for her of the writers and artists, memories of creative geniuses from the past that became as inseparable from the pathways and sand dunes of Carmel as the familiar fog.

And from her Irish ancestors Peggy had inherited an impish side, and the ability to laugh at herself, especially when she felt she had become overly dramatic, which was often. She spouted lofty quotations and admonitions without embarrassment because that side of her nature was balanced by a huge enjoyment in poking fun at herself.

No wonder, then, that Susan's sheltered childhood permitted her to live her first seventeen years as a precocious, adventuresome dreamer, nestled in a secure and beautiful world. School life also seemed charmed. She and her young classmates moved into high school as an eager, noisy troupe. Hers was a course set along a silvery pathway, allowing the carefree Susan to dream her dreams and assume a future that would be richly rewarding and serenely simple.

That was before Chad. She didn't hate Chad for what he did, in fact some years afterward, Susan realized the accomplishments and successes of her adult life stemmed directly from that incident. He rocked her boat, forced her off course, shaking away all illusions. That night forced her to lay to rest the silly daydreaming, and toughened her to withstand the realities of life.

Chad, her knight in shining armor. They grew up neighbors and pals, then they were the most handsome couple in high school. Susan envisioned them spending their lives together, there was never any doubt in her mind. Until that night.

Their Senior Prom was a much-anticipated affair. Everyone in the class worked carwashes and bake sales until they could afford to rent the fashionable Pebble Beach Racquet Club for the dance. The impressive locale automatically demanded that dresses be a little more extravagant, everything just a bit more sophisticated. The weeks before were a whirl of activity for Susan. She chose a dress that caused her mother a little concern—she felt it made her daughter look years older. But the prom was at the Club. You couldn't go in some frilly adolescent thing! It took her a week of desperate conversations with her girlfriends and mother to decide what to do with her hair. All the planning was worth it when she readied herself for the dance. Chad had his parents' car for the occasion, and sat with her parents for a while making small talk while Susan fussed with last minute adjustments to her hair and gown. After the required prom night photographs were taken by her proud father, they waltzed out of the house, beautiful, young and innocent.

When Susan pried her bedroom window open in the early hours of the next morning to try to get home without facing her desperately worried parents, she was black and blue, the once picture-perfect dress torn, and her sweet innocence having suffered a broadside blow of devastating proportions. Every fantasy in her head had been blown apart by the person she trusted most. Chad had suddenly changed from her friend and sweetheart into a rough, uncaring monster, insisting they were going to do what they had coyly referred to as 'going all the way.' "That's for when we get married," Susan had said over their years of going steady, and Chad always agreed. But tonight he had asked her outside for a romantic walk through the spectacular grounds, and under the starry sky while they gazed at a perfect full moon, dramatically shadowed by the stark branches of cypress trees, the familiar, reliable Chad was gone, all pretense removed. He allowed no time for her agreement or acceptance. This was going to be the place and time. When she pleaded with him, she learned that brute strength would win despite whatever words of respect and love had passed between them. Chad was going to rape her.

And he would have, if two chaperones hadn't walked into the garden just a few feet from the secluded pathway where Chad had pulled Susan. It was close enough to make the boy think they'd be discovered, so he pushed Susan quickly along the rocky path and out into the parking lot, where he forced her into his car and sped away. The disturbance had soured his sexual excitement, leaving him embarrassed and gushing forth apologies—'Didn't know what got into him, could she ever forgive him'—'Let's just forget it, like it never happened'—'He respected her, how could she doubt that.' When Susan sat cold and silent, refusing to respond to Chad's pleas for forgiveness, his temper rose, his anger measured by the weight of his foot on the gas pedal as he slammed the car through winding Pebble Beach roadways, berating her as a silly, immature kid who should have grown up long ago. "You might think you're a fairy princess, but you're just another stupid broad," was the way he summed it up, punctuating his words with hard jabs to her face, arms and chest.

*The end of a beautiful romance*, thought Susan, overcoming pain and humiliation with the realistic humor learned from her Mother. But it marked the end of her life as a "fairy princess." The wonder was that she didn't become bitter, just determined and realistic. The rock solid decision she made was that the dreaming was over, and she would apply herself to accomplishing whatever she decided to do with her life. No more cozy cottages and picket fences, but a real plan for college and then law school. Hard as flint when it came to succeeding at school and then establishing her place in the law, she rose to the top.

Susan shook her head as she broke the spell of her reminiscences. *So after all that hard work to get where I am, where am I going, and why am I so damned lonely all of a sudden?* She looked at the unused yellow pad and slowly wrote, 'One hell of a mess!' and then went off to bed.

In the privacy of their bedrooms that night each of them marked the emotional evening with a decision as to where they wanted their life to go. Allison knew she would call Joe as many times as it took to convince him to take part in repairing what was happening to them. She knew him to his very soul. Eventually he would pry off this stubborn envelope of secrecy and anger and deal with the situation with honesty. For good or for bad. She would begin tomorrow night.

Glynnis felt uncharacteristically motherly. Each of her companions was battling a desperate crisis, relegating her own feelings of insecurity and worthlessness to selfish trifles. Perhaps there was no way to help, but she'd do whatever possible. One thing was obvious. It was time to stop expecting other people to hold her hand so she could just make it through a normal day. *Imagine not even being able to choose what fish to order for lunch! I've been a calamity, a disgrace. But no more. Starting tomorrow, no more.*

Susan was relieved she didn't have to live with a secret any longer. Having declared it openly, it was time to do some hard thinking. She must call Philip. But first she needed to talk to Mother. She'd call early tomorrow morning.

## Chapter Six

# Wednesday

**Instinct shook Susan** from sleep at four thirty the next morning. Accounting for the difference in time in San Francisco, she'd catch Mother sitting at her desk in the sunroom upstairs, reading Irish poetry while enjoying Earl Grey tea in her favorite cup, delicate white porcelain strewn with green shamrocks. "If I were to neglect my morning ritual for even one day I would forever lose every trace of my Hibernian roots," Peggy had once told Susan gravely. "Besides, up here I don't have to interrupt my peace to help your father find the 'this' and the 'that' he inevitably misplaces every morning!"

Susan smiled as she remembered this scene, and the inevitable twinkle in her mother's eye. She already knew how she'd handle the call to prevent it from slipping too far into whimsy. When Peggy answered the phone her reaction was one of delight at the sound of her daughter's voice. "Darling, I can't wait to hear about all you've been doing. And of course any and all gossip!"

Susan took firm control. "Hello, Mother. It's so good to talk to you, but I can't really chat this time. I've got something I need to discuss. Something important."

Peggy Michaels understood immediately and dropped the levity. "I'm here, Susan. Go ahead."

The young woman outlined to her mother what had happened between Philip and her, why she had gone to Hawaii, the discovery of her pregnancy, her decision to have an abortion, and the realization that she couldn't take that step without more thought. Susan had no difficulty describing the situation clearly and fully without wasted words, without embarrassment. Her voice was subdued by the gravity of what she was relating, but she was in control of her emotions. Coming to the end, she sighed. "I'm going to call Philip tonight. This is about him, too, and it's not fair that he doesn't know, can't have a say. I just wanted to talk to you first, Mother."

"I'm so glad you did call, Susan. You know me, and understand I'm here for you, but also I respect the fact that this is your life and your decision. If I can help, I will do so with love."

"The thing that's been troubling me is this. How did I get so turned away from what most women would look upon as a natural and fulfilling part of their life? I used to dream of the day I'd be married, have children. But now I can't imagine changing the way my life is when I've worked so hard to get here. How did I get on such a single-minded track?"

"You know, dear, your decision to become a lawyer, and to excel, was admirable. And you were right to work so hard to achieve your success. I wouldn't have you change a minute of it. But your determination developed because of a grotesque incident in your young life. Funny, it's the one time we never really talked much, but it was apparent to me that you needed your privacy. And you handled it with so much wisdom and poise, I knew you'd be all right. Yet sometimes when we draw up all our willpower to move beyond a roadblock in a new direction, it's easier if we close as many windows to the past as we can. There's a metaphor lurking in my mind about pulling the drawbridge that spans the moat between cold, dark night and bright new day—but now's not the time for metaphors." She laughed gently and paused.

"Of course you've stayed the loving, sweet person you always were. But maybe there was a little defiance in your decision to put career first. You'd been hurt deeply by someone you trusted, and it sent your dreams careening down. Perhaps it was too hard to keep that unquestioning trust and those sweet dreams." Peggy remembered so vividly the trauma of that incident, how she had wanted to protect her daughter, but knew instinctively that Susan needed her love and loyalty, but wanted to develop her own answer to the insult directed at her pride and her heart. "You just may have shut some doors you didn't intend to close."

Fundamental to Susan's legal identity was the knowledge that she should listen carefully to what others had to say and weigh their opinions without allowing personal feelings to interfere. There were kernels of truth and valuable insights to be gained, even if she disagreed with the conclusion. So as she listened, she shook her head in agreement, realizing the assessment was so. "Yes, I know what you're saying. But it's been many years. If there was anger involved in my actions, that dissipated long ago. I have nothing to prove to anybody anymore. I simply love my work. And my lifestyle. When I meet with friends socially we have great discussions and arguments covering any number of subjects, but Johnny's new tooth or Suzie's latest cute saying are not part of it."

Her mother's voice was kind. "Are none of your friends married then, Susan?"

"Well, of course some are. A lot are divorced, too. And heavens, Mother, I could certainly enjoy marriage. I wanted to marry Philip, remember? Having a family, that's where it got sticky."

Patiently, "So none of your friends have children?"

Susan had to chuckle. Her mother was good at this! "Yes, some have families. Okay, they're able to handle it. I'm just not. They must talk about baby clothes and immunization records from eight to five and spend the evening hours thinking like adults. I guess they're more adaptable to different situations. They can change gears."

"Oh, well, now that you mention it, I have always noticed your rather plodding nature, darling." Peggy attempted to sound serious as she teased.

"All right, Mother, 'Uncle.' I don't know why I can't envision motherhood as part of my life. I think, though, that it's instinct or intuition. I have simply believed it's not for me. But I am having trouble with this decision. I'm not trying to be selfish; I want to do the right thing. I'm standing at a fork in the road that is a real powerhouse. Can I go on with the world set up the way I've chosen, or do I need to revisit just who I am and what I'm all about?"

"Dearest daughter, you couldn't be selfish. Resolute, even stubborn. But selfish, never. Don't be too hard on yourself. You've moved ahead into areas where women of my generation had difficulty going, perhaps didn't even want to go. It's no wonder the road is rocky." Peggy Michaels smiled wistfully. "I remember when you were tiny you were fascinated by Aunt Maureen's antique hand mirror. You know, the silver one with flowers and fairies wrought into the handle and frame. You'd spend hours looking at yourself, imagining and dreaming. Do you recall what you told me on one of those visits? You gazed into the mirror and then at me and said, 'Mother, I want to be as pretty as I am in here.' I don't know what made me think of that right now. Just that you've always been one with your feet on the ground and head in the clouds, I suppose."

"I don't like to feel sorry for myself, but I must admit to a tinge of jealousy. Here I am surrounded by this gnarly mess. Why couldn't my life be like yours? You and Father love each other, always have, always will. Your married life is a joy to behold, so beautifully simple, why shouldn't I be jealous!" Troubled though she was, a loving smile bathed Susan's face.

After a stillness that was worrisome, her mother spoke. "Sweet Susan, you are perfectly right, of course. Your father and I love each other immensely and always will. But no one's life is a journey without moments of bleakness and trouble." Peggy hesitated, then continued quietly.

"When Paul and I were newly married, living in San Francisco as we do again now, he spoiled me terribly. Still does, of course. From the very start, if I glanced twice at something in a store window, next evening he would bring it home. No matter how tired after a day of work, he would revive and take me to the ballet or opera or a concert. He spent three months locating an out-of-print book of Irish folklore I had mentioned. He told me his greatest pleasure was in pleasing me.

"Except in one desire. I wanted to be an actress. Paul was adamantly opposed. He thought I'd be traveling all over the planet, and he'd be ignored. Well, I did everything I could to get my way, even stamped my foot and pouted until he relented and told me to try. I did just that, and had some success locally in a couple of productions. I was offered a leading role in a play in Los Angeles, and of course that fanned my ego.

Your father couldn't help but tell me this was just what he'd feared, I'd be on the road and he'd be alone. But I convinced him that if I could go just this one time, it would quench my thirst for stardom and I'd settle down. Amid great grumbling and grouching, he agreed. It was to be six months that I'd be away, but he would come to L.A. on weekends as often as he could. I made arrangements to stay with my aunt and off I went. It was more difficult than I'd imagined to leave Paul and go off alone, and many times I thought about quitting and going home. But I'd made such a scene, and I really did want to have my name up in lights. So I stuck with it.

"After I'd been away a couple of weeks I discovered I was pregnant. I persuaded the producer to let me take a quick trip to the City to tell your Father. We were overwhelmed with happiness. I rushed back to work, hardly able to wait until I could return and get ready for the baby. Paul lectured me constantly to take care of myself and not overwork. But production was far behind schedule and the pressure mounted. We worked hard and I got little rest. One month after returning to Los Angeles I miscarried."

Susan heard nothing from the other end of the line, only felt the heavy silence. "Oh, Mother. I'm so sorry. I always knew there was something. But I never imagined what had happened. How did you ever survive?"

Peggy's voice was slowed by the memory. "It was unbelievably sad. I was grief-stricken, but your father was totally destroyed. First we consoled one another, or tried to. But then it was like a cold fog swept between us. He blamed me, although he never said such a thing. I knew it, though, and understood, because I blamed myself, too. There was nothing I could do, and we grew further and further apart. We never said a mean word to each other. Just went through one gray day after another. I began to think this would be our life forever. And then there came a morning when things weren't quite as bad. I began to notice the beauty that was around me, and Paul seemed to take interest in his work again. One evening after dinner as we sat on the terrace, your father reached over and took my hand, and I knew we'd found our way through the endless dark caverns of despair and were going to be all right. And we were. Soon after, I became pregnant again. Paul insisted we had to get out of the city, designed our wonderful home in Carmel, and when it was finished we moved there, where I spent those months being coddled and catered to until you were born, beautiful, graceful, wise and the most delightful baby the world had ever seen. And because we knew the bottomless sorrow of loss, you were all the more precious to us."

"Mom, I'm sorry I caused you to revisit all this. I'm sorry to phone home with a heart-wrenching problem instead of just filling your ears with joy. But I appreciate that you would tell me. It helps. Thank you for your love and support. You don't have any tricks that guarantee a life of happiness do you?"

"A sense of humor helps immensely, my dear." And tears splashed into the now-cold cup of Earl Gray tea in the sunroom in San Francisco.

Bed felt inviting to Susan as she slipped back for a few more hours of sleep. It was just after five o'clock. She was relaxed after the phone call and quickly fell asleep.

The day was delightful as Susan wandered over a grassy field. Although it was lush and green, it was definitely not the Islands. It seemed more like California. Perhaps the Gold Country. She thought at first it was Hawaii because of all the palm trees, but apparently they were valley oaks, or at least now they were. Off in the distance she saw Mother dressed in a long flowered skirt, white petticoat showing beneath, a black lace shawl covering her head and shoulders. She carried the large flat wicker basket Susan recognized as the one Mother used for gathering flowers from her cutting garden. She stopped now and then to pick up a small animal—a tiny rabbit, pink piglets, a kitten. From the branch of an old oak she lifted a nest of featherless baby birds. She noticed her daughter across the field and waved. Susan ran through the grass to meet her, and arm in arm they moved to the edge of the hilltop where Mother put her basket down and Susan quickly tipped it up, sending dozens of little animals tumbling down the bank. The women sat down under a tree and both were crying. But then Susan opened her briefcase, which apparently she'd been carrying, brought out a legal brief, and began to read aloud. Mother nodded and smiled, but as she listened she reached deep into what had been a shallow basket to lift out a small bundle wrapped in soft blankets.

"That's wonderful, dear, but what shall we do with this little one?"

Susan pulled back the soft woolen blanket and smiled at the red-faced baby inside. "I don't know, Mother. He was supposed to go with all the others. Why do you suppose he wanted to stay?"

"Lonesome, I think," Peggy Michaels said. When Susan tried to answer, she realized Mother was gone and she was alone with the child.

It was an odd and cryptic dream, but surprisingly not an unsettling one.

After showering and dressing, Susan looked at herself in the mirror, feeling unexpectedly relaxed and comfortable. She felt capable of a decision, ready to take control of her life once more. "What a difference a day makes!" she laughed to herself.

Glynnis and Allison were already in the living room when she approached, and her improved color and bright smile as she greeted them signaled she was doing better, and they were pleased.

As ideas were discussed for the day's activity Susan, noticing some threatening clouds, turned on the television for a weather check. They were watching for the latest update when the housekeeper came in carrying a large brown manila package.

"Oh, Noelani, something for me?" Susan smiled and reached for the envelope.

"No, Miss Michaels. It's addressed to Miss Paxton." Noelani handed the parcel to a curious Glynnis and left.

"Now, that's a surprise. Whatever could it be?" Glynnis scanned the address and registered understanding. "Oh, of course. It's from Uncle John. He must have sent me papers to sign regarding Father's estate. It's certainly large, though. Maybe he shipped us some of my favorite lobster from Bookbinders Restaurant!" She laughed as her fingers worked at opening the wrapping. As she pulled the paper back, a puzzling array met her eyes: a small package wrapped in a soft papery cloth decorated with a bold brown and black design, a very old and worn red lacquer box, and two envelopes. Glynnis recognized the handwriting on the top envelope as John Halverson's. She opened the letter and read his short note.

*Glynnis dear,*

*Just a few days before your father's death he directed me to arrange your trip to Hawaii and then to send this package to you.*

*The contents of the parcel will be, I believe, self-explanatory and will answer the many questions I'm sure you have at this moment.*

*My duty to Edward and to you was to bring you to this moment—to set the stage, so to speak. Any more writing by me would be superfluous, other than to offer my apologies for sending you on this journey, I know, against your wishes. I trust the information now in your hands will explain what must have appeared to be overbearing meddling on my part.*

*Please call me soon, Glynnis, so I can be assured you are all right. As your godfather I feel responsible for your welfare, and truly care about you. With my affection, John Halverson.*

Nervously Glynnis surveyed the remaining items. The other letter, addressed to her, bore her father's handwriting. Wary about opening the enigmatic letter, she looked toward her friends.

"It seems Father arranged for me to receive this package—for me to be here to receive it. I have to tell you I'm a little unnerved by all of this. I just don't understand why . . ."

"Look, we'll cancel today's plans. Susan and I can just sunbathe here in the garden while you go through your mail. We don't need to go out every day." Allison smiled warmly, hoping to alleviate Glynnis' nervousness.

Calming words from her friend buoyed Glynnis and she straightened to look from Allison to Susan. "Don't fret about me. This has taken the wind out of my sails temporarily, but it's quite all right. I want you two to go ahead and go out, but I need to stay here and find out what this is all about.

"Allison's right, you know. We'd be perfectly comfortable staying here." Susan had reservations about leaving, seeing that Glynnis was obviously disturbed and confused. "No wonder you're puzzled. That's a mystery box if ever there was one." Susan surveyed the strange array that had arrived out of the blue.

"No, really I'd rather stay alone. I need to be by myself, if you don't mind. Please go off and don't worry about me." Strangely, Glynnis did want privacy. "It helps to know you care. I'll be fine."

After Susan and Allison rounded up their gear and reluctantly drove off, Glynnis carried the contents of the package into the private, enclosed garden just off her bedroom. It had become a favorite spot where she could sit each morning before leaving her quarters. The Koolau Mountains moved her more deeply than anything else on the Island—more than anything she had ever seen. They were ageless, haunting, fascinating. And the garden itself was so quiet, so lovely. Her nerves calmed by the tranquility, she took a seat on the bench, picked up her father's letter and opened it.

The crisp onionskin paper crackled as she unfolded the thick stack of pages, each covered with the spidery handwriting of her father so familiar to Glynnis. Her fingers moved lovingly across the words, as if stroking her father's cheek. Tears sprang to her eyes as she began to read.

*Dearest Glynnis,*

*My dear friend John Halverson has promised that after my death he will arrange for you to vacation in Hawaii, and once you have been there long enough to acclimate yourself a bit, he will send this packet to you. Therefore, dearest daughter, if you are reading these words, I am gone and you are suddenly alone.*

*Do not grieve too much over my passing. I have had a full life and I am at peace about dying. My only concern is for you, my child. All your life you have been a loyal, dutiful daughter, but as a consequence, you've sacrificed your own personal dreams and aspirations—your independence. I worry that I should not have allowed you to be so selfless, and I wonder how you will adapt now to a different life. I have felt helpless that I will not be able to help you adjust.*

*But there is something I can do for you, dearest, that may in some way enlighten you and give you courage to live happily in the years to come. I want you to know something about me—a part of my life story that only a handful of people know. Believe me when I tell you that this secrecy was not born of embarrassment or regret, but because I felt it was kinder to the people I loved and cared about most. Perhaps I erred. Who's to say? Life passes so quickly, and when we stand near the end and look back, it is quite easy to scold ourselves and find fault without remembering that some of our decisions were made by a much younger person. Oh, to have the vigor and dreams of our youth while simultaneously enjoying the wisdom that comes with age.*

*So I will proceed, hoping you relate this story to the thoughts and actions of the young man that I was when it occurred.*

*After the outbreak of World War II I attempted to enlist in the Army, but a pesky heart condition prevented me from serving my country. I therefore pursued my education, attended Yale as Father had, and graduated with a Masters in Business in 1947. This you already know. Mother and Father rewarded me with a trip to Hawaii for my graduation present. It didn't take long to convince my good friend John Halverson, your Uncle John, to go with me. John was a little older than I and received his law degree at the same time I earned my B.A. We were fraternity brothers—roommates, in fact—and inseparable.*

Studied hard, of course, but we also pulled some of the usual college pranks together, I must admit.

Father was already planning my entrance into the family firm, which was what I had been working to achieve, of course, but I wanted a little time when I could throw off all the plans and expectations. Be a gypsy, go native, if you will. Perhaps it seemed like a chance for one final fling. And so the two of us set off, ready for a real adventure.

Life in our Pennsylvania is fairly staid, as you well know, Glynnis. So believe me, Hawaii fulfilled every wild imagining we had. Our accommodations were at the Royal Hawaiian Hotel, that most glorious landmark. We spent our days on the beach at Waikiki, swimming, soaking in the sun on the warm sand, watching the Hawaiian lads on their long surfboards. What amazing athletes they were. I must also confess that, being healthy young men, we spent some time watching the beautiful girls. In those days most of the people on the beach were Hawaiians, not tourists, and we marveled how the mixture of ancestries flowed into such perfect beauty in the Island women.

One day two lovely girls attracted our attention. They sat together laughing and talking with warmth and gaiety. And they were so beautiful. John and I introduced ourselves. They were intrigued by two boys from the East, and smiled shyly, introducing themselves as sisters, Alesa and Emma. We four sat on the sand and talked for hours until sunset. Parting as the day ended, we arranged to meet again the following day.

And so it went. John and Emma were very attracted to each other while Alesa filled my thoughts all day and my dreams all night. And she seemed to like me.

As I continue, my daughter, I hope you will not find my actions repugnant. That I acted contra to society's teachings, I admit. But my intentions were honest and my emotions true.

It had become a habit for our foursome to buy fruit and hot cooked meats from a food stand and eat dinner on the beach at sunset. Then the girls would hurry home and we would return to our hotel. But one night we waited to view the full moon. It was glorious, cutting a silver path through the water. And as it grew dark we knew without words being spoken that we would not separate that night. Alesa and I shared the hotel room while John secured separate accommodations for himself and Emma.

The following days passed blissfully, and as the end of our vacation neared both John and I determined we would not go home. Of course there were violent protestations from Mother and Father, but there was little they could do from such a distance. I learned later they concocted a story that I was gaining great experience in an old, very reputable accounting firm in Honolulu. This face-saving alibi contained a thread of truth, since I did take a position as mailboy in that firm! But the story shielded my parents from humiliation and that seemed to be enough to overcome their uneasiness, their embarrassment.

We were so very happy, Glynnis. Alesa was an artist and worked in a small studio. When I wasn't working, I would watch her for hours while she painted. She even painted my portrait, and made me look handsome! We had very little money, but I splurged one payday and purchased a small book written by Don Blanding, an author who wrote romantic poetry about the Islands he loved. The volume was called <u>Vagabond's House</u>. You'll find it in the packet that you just received. As you read the poems I hope you feel their beauty as we did. The two of us sat for hours reading passages to one another, dreaming of our future together.

We saw John and Emma often, picnicking and partying together. One evening, after we'd been in Hawaii about a year, they announced they were going to be married. How we celebrated that night! And in the following weeks Alesa helped Emma plan her wedding. Their mother worked happily with them, also. What a noble lady she was. She understood her daughters loving these 'foreigners' and blessed John and Emma's wedding. But if she wished her other daughter, my Alesa, could also be properly married, she never made comment to me or criticized either of us.

And so the ceremony took place. I must tell you that as John wed his love, I felt twinges of discomfort. Why didn't I make the same commitment to Alesa? I loved her. She was my life. Why couldn't I ask her to marry me? But I rationalized that John was a few years my senior. I imagined it was natural that he desired to settle down before I did. I smile now at how easily I fooled myself, and in the process, exonerated myself.

Now Glynnis, you know me as a very orderly, responsible businessman, and it may be hard for you to comprehend how quickly two years went by while I shuffled along at a low-level job and allowed this relationship to progress aimlessly, without design. I understand if you are surprised. It surprises me now. But they were days filled with love and the excitement of being in love in a beautiful land.

Toward the end of the second year, Emma told us she and John were expecting a child. Alesa cried with happiness for her sister and I suddenly saw so clearly I was denying her the dignified, orderly life and happiness she deserved—that I must stand up and do the right thing. But it was extremely difficult to make such a move. For the first time I realized the importance of my family, their expectations for me, my responsibility to them, my desire to succeed and be in the company of my own people. I missed that part of my life. But I loved Alesa.

So one night we talked, and I tried to explain my dilemma. I asked her to marry me and described how we would go to Philadelphia where we would be happy, I would be successful, and we would have children. Everything would be right and good.

*The silence that followed my proposal spanned eons. I finally forced myself to look into the face of my Hawaiian love. She was smiling wistfully, tears flowing silently down her face. Alesa assured me of her love for me, yet she understood the life we'd dreamed of together would never succeed. She would perish and die if I took her to the East; her heart belonged in the Islands. Nor did she believe she would be warmly received by my family and friends. She was not bitter, simply resigned. Intelligent enough to realize the obvious.*

*I protested. Determined now that I could not lose her, I implored her that if she wouldn't go with me, I would chuck it all, stay with her there and we would be forever happy.*

*She gently stroked my hair as a mother would soothe a child and as she quietly continued, I felt my dreams shatter, the truth of what she said undeniable. I could not cast aside my heritage any more than she could hers. Although I had basked in the beauty of the Islands, there was a distant call to return to my roots and continue with my life plan, and the time to do that was now.*

*My dear, it is painful to examine these memories in depth as I do now. So let me finish quickly.*

*Through tears and wrenching sorrow we parted. I returned to Philadelphia, started my career with Father, and soon life took on the normalcy that characterized the rest of my days. I became engaged to your dear Mother, and we were wed. Your birth four years later filled us both with happiness.*

*Although ours was not a passionate marriage, your Mother and I loved one another and were loyal partners. I confess that throughout my life I secretly maintained what became a rich, rewarding friendship with Alesa. We corresponded over the years, exchanging good and bad news, pictures of our families, sharing our life stories. But we never met again.*

*If you are puzzled about John, let me explain his story. Some time after I returned home he sent word that Emma had died giving birth to his son, Timothy. John was devastated. He attempted to rear the boy, but without his beloved Emma it was hopeless. Hawaii now broke his heart. He knew he must return to Philadelphia and get on with his life, and although it hurt him to the quick, he left his infant boy with Alesa and her mother so that Timothy would be loved and cared for in his home, Hawaii.*

*And so, my precious, I have come to the end. This is another inheritance that I leave you—one that will, I hope, encourage you to reach out for adventure, even if you risk making mistakes. You are careful and responsible. I do not imagine you will duplicate the foolish errors of your father. But do taste the wonders of life, see the beauty. Touch people and let them touch you. The rewards will be more valuable than the money you inherit.*

*Enclosed in this packet is the Blanding booklet, wrapped in a small piece of tapa cloth which I kept as a reminder of the home Alesa and I kept together. We purchased a large roll of the cloth from an old Hawaiian vendor on King Street and used it lavishly to decorate our small home. It was the first purchase for our dreamed-of 'Vagabond's House.' The carved box contains a seed lei that Alesa presented me on my birthday. She knew the old woman who sewed those shiny brown seeds into intricate patterns, and even helped her make it. We had the enclosed photograph taken on that very birthday night. As you see, I wore the lei with great delight! The pressed flowers were gathered in our garden during those happy days. Faded now, but still vivid and fragrant in my memory.*

*I have written a last letter to Alesa, who still resides in Honolulu, explaining that I am confiding our secret to you. You will find her address in the box, also. I know you may hesitate, but I urge you to meet*

*her. In doing so you will fulfill your father's dream, but more impor-*
*tantly, I am certain you two will love each other.*

*I pray for years filled with joy and happiness for you, dear Glynnis.*
*Your loving father, Edward Paxton.*

Upon reaching the end and reading her father's signature, Glynnis was suddenly bolted back to the present. The letter rustled in her shaking hands as her feelings vaulted between confusion, denial, embarrassment and the undeniable knowledge that what she just read was true. There was no reason for Father to write this history for her if it weren't. A lifetime of memories flooded in. Nothing that she knew of him related to the young man she'd just read about. But indeed he was that boy, youthful, carefree, unworried about life's responsibilities.

For a long time Glynnis cried. She cried for her father, for her mother who had been deceived throughout her marriage. And she cried for Alesa, for the two lovers who lost their chance for bliss. She cried for John Halverson, for his infant son who was virtually orphaned, for his wife who died so young. But mostly she cried for herself, for reasons so diverse and bewildering she could only succumb to the self-indulgence without analyzing why. How could she be required to deal with such news? Her orderly life was being destroyed. Didn't Father feel humiliated confessing these indiscretions to his own daughter? No, that wasn't what hurt her. Didn't he feel ashamed for not revealing this to her before, for not helping her learn from his experience to broaden her horizons and enjoy more of life?

Glynnis almost relished the bitterness and disappointment she allowed to pull her toward defeat. No wonder her life was pathetic. She could never hope to overcome what had been done to her. How foolish it had been to entertain for even a few days the possibility of turning over a new leaf. As she sobbed, she looked again at the words her father had written to her. Startled suddenly, she grasped how difficult it must have been for him to do this. He didn't have to. His secret could have died with him. What a sacrifice this was. Most certainly he must have worried that she would turn in anger from him instead of learning what he so desperately needed to impart to her. More than all the years of loving upbringing, this was his greatest gift.

Slowly, with a deeper level of understanding, Glynnis reread the long letter, listening to the messages her father had left for her, with compassion and acceptance. After reading the last page, she picked up each of the other items, holding them, trying to imagine her father and his beloved sitting together, reading poetry, laughing, celebrating birthdays, dreaming their dreams, crying when they reached the end. The photo portrayed a happy young couple, love shining in their faces.

Glynnis straightened, dabbed her face to wipe away the tears and nodded resolutely. "I will go to see Alesa."

## Chapter Seven

# Later Wednesday

**Shuffling through the** packet of papers, Glynnis located Alesa's address and telephone number. With unexpected resolve, she lifted the receiver and telephoned this woman who had suddenly become part of her life. Each ring jangled her, but she resisted the urge to hang up, and finally a woman's voice responded. "Hello?" Glynnis suddenly had no voice, and after a long pause the melodic, Hawaiian voice at the other end of the line spoke again. "Hello? This is Alesa. Who is calling me? Please answer if you are there."

"I'm Glynnis. Glynnis Paxton. I thought I should call." Her hands were shaking, her breath coming in ragged spurts that tightened her chest, but she continued weakly.

"Oh,—oh, Glynnis! Darling Glynnis. I've wanted so much for so long to see you. I knew you were to be in the Islands— your father wrote me before he . . ." She paused, then continued quietly. "This is hard for us both, isn't it? I worried that you would not call. I would have understood if you had not."

Glynnis listened, fascinated, trying to relate this voice to her father, to herself. "I don't know if I should have called. It is probably a silly idea. But it was Father's wish. You'll have to forgive me, it must be such an imposition. You don't even know me. I'm quite bewildered."

"Please, don't hang up or anything. Don't hang up. I prayed you'd call me. Your father wanted that, and I did, too. And don't feel awkward. I'm just an old Hawaiian lady who has wanted to know you, to see you, for so long." Alesa paused momentarily, and when she spoke again there was strength and warmth in her gentle voice. "You know the story of your father and me now, and so you must know that we loved each other once. Well, that love changed to a deep friendship between us. I've heard all about you—loved you—since your birth. I feel like your Auntie. But we mustn't waste this time talking on the telephone. Come to my house, please. Then we can truly get to know each other. Do come right away!"

"I will, Mrs. . . Miss. . ." Glynnis felt foolish stammering, not knowing how to address this lady who reacted to her so kindly.

"Just call me Alesa. And don't worry about anything. By the time we've talked a few minutes, we'll be like old friends. I promise."

After hanging up, Glynnis felt panicky. How would she get there? The driver, Eric, was responsible and friendly, and had helped with their transportation so far, and it would relieve some of the tension to have him accompany her, but she didn't feel she should use the condo car. She decided to ask him to call a taxi for her. He phoned a friend who drove cab, which relaxed her somewhat since she could be almost certain she wasn't risking life and limb. Glynnis went to her room to freshen up, not sure what to wear, what to do. She chose a calf-length circular skirt of soft gray-blue with a blouse of dusty gold, adding some large antique blue clay beads. She scribbled a short note for her friends: 'Left on business. Be back before dinner or I will call you.' It didn't adequately explain the situation, and probably wouldn't put their minds completely at ease, but it was impossible to organize her thoughts and clearly describe what was taking her away. *I'll explain everything tonight. If I survive the day, that is*, she muttered to herself as she patted her hair, smoothed the skirt, and glanced in the mirror one last time to make sure she was presentable.

Seated nervously in the back seat of the taxi a few minutes later, Glynnis leaned forward stiffly in the back seat, hand braced against the door for support. There were no coherent thoughts, only wispy fragments which intertwined with visual input as they moved across town. It was much like a movie nightmare scene where people's faces looked at the camera through distorting mirrors and colors were primary and much too bright. Sometimes everything moved in ultra-slow motion, and she noted tiny details—facial expressions of pedestrians, the texture of the pavement, traffic and "For Sale" signs, neighborhood pets that ambled along the sidewalks. Then the car hurtled at violent speed through traffic, and everything was a blur. Strangely, that didn't alarm her. She simply noticed how quickly things whipped past the window and thought it odd. Glynnis had planned to use the travel time to formulate an approach to this unusual meeting, to get her thoughts together, gather her courage. Instead she was floating in limbo, not finding it important to anticipate what was going to happen, or perhaps refusing to deal with it.

The driver spoke to her several times over his shoulder, commenting on the traffic or the weather—casual and polite chit-chat that Glynnis answered without thought. It startled her, then, when she realized he had said something of more import that she hadn't caught, and when he turned around to look carefully at her, she realized that the car was stopped.

"You okay, lady? We're here. You want some help, yeah? It's a real haul up those stairs, man."

Glynnis was jarred back to her surroundings. "Oh, of course we're here. Thanks, but I'm fine. I don't need help." As the driver came around and opened the door, she paid him and stepped out to find herself in a very old residential district, the houses clinging to a steep hill. The gardens were well established, all awash with colorful blooms cascading down and ropy vines twining their way up to, and even through, the treetops. A mailbox hand-painted with leaves and Alesa's house number stood next to a well-worn flight of wooden steps. Glynnis' eyes moved from the bottom upward, following the turns and landings, until she gazed at the entryway. A petite woman with steely gray hair wearing a dark wine-colored muu-muu trimmed in white lace leaned over the railing of the balcony, excited movements telegraphing her joy, a tiny tropical bird flitting amid the colorful foliage.

"Here I am, my dear, up here! Hurry up the stairs!" As she spoke, the little lady waved frantically, bursting with anticipation and excitement.

Glynnis was captivated by the unembarrassed happiness of this woman and she responded with honest pleasure and an unaccustomed feeling of familiarity. "Hello, Alesa. I'm coming right up. There's lots of stairs!"

"That's what keeps me young. But you be careful. The steps are old, and some of them are a little wobbly." When Glynnis approached the last landing and final run of stairs, Alesa could wait no longer, and rushed to meet her.

The older Hawaiian hugged and kissed the young Philadelphia girl, took her hand and patted it, kissed it, cradled it. She cupped Glynnis' face with hands that were graceful and gentle, but weathered by work and tropical sun. Her hands smoothed the younger woman's hair carefully, though not a hair seemed out of place. The tiny Alesa stepped back, and with wide, bright eyes, a glorious smile and outstretched arms welcomed this tall and beautiful young woman.

"I've known you since the day you were born, my dear. You have been in my heart all these years, just as though you'd been—as though you'd been a keiki, a child, here." Alesa hesitated, a look of concern crossing her lined, brown face. "Of course, I felt like your Auntie, loving you and proud of you like any Auntie would be. I hope you understand."

Glynnis nodded, emotion choking off her voice. Instantly she was embraced by loving arms again, as Alesa steered her toward the house.

Tears pooled in the older woman's eyes as she pulled at Glynnis' arm, ushering her into the living room. "Come in. Come into my home and from this moment on, you think of it as your home, too. Wherever you are, whether you're here or far away, you will always have a loving home here. Thank you for coming. It couldn't have been easy."

Glynnis scanned the warm, friendly room, finding each nook crowded with paintings, photographs, floral arrangements. There were displays of trinkets, seashells, driftwood. A low table held stacks of photo albums. The furniture was well worn, but richly crafted. She immediately felt at home here. There was no pretense. The beauty came from within the heart and the talent of the woman standing beside her. As you studied the decor, you knew the mistress of the house.

"You have a wonderful home. Have you always lived here?"

The house and the dear Hawaiian woman were linked in Glynnis' mind. Alesa's essence flowed into the place.

"It seems like always," Alesa laughed. "I've been here since your—what I mean is, right after your father—oh, my. This is foolish. I have been blessed with your visit and must not waste your precious time with my embarrassed hesitation. I want you to enjoy yourself and get to know me a little. This flightiness is so unlike me."

"Alesa, you're looking at someone who was born flighty!" Glynnis laughed. Why was it she felt so comfortable here? This had to be the most awkward situation she had ever faced. But her father's story had moved her, and this gentle woman was as easy and satisfying to be with as a favorite book. And the room. She looked around at Alesa's home, the spilt-out soul and emotions of an artist. Yet Glynnis thought it somehow captured her own feelings, as well.

She paused suddenly, horrified. She had been swayed by all of this so easily. It must have been the tale of love in a tropic land, a land she was visiting herself, that had overcome her sense of propriety. Getting too familiar and comfortable would be disloyal to Mother's memory. She must brace up a little and act in a way appropriate to the moment—no more, no less. Polite, but with some semblance of aloofness. Glynnis stiffened imperceptibly.

"But you're entirely correct, a little embarrassment is understandable. Of course, you'd be uncomfortable. This is quite extraordinary, to say the least." Glynnis felt she'd regained status for her mother without being rude.

Although she still smiled, there was an unmistakable hurt in Alesa's eyes before she turned her head and gazed into the distance briefly. When she looked at Glynnis again it was with dignity and composure. "Oh, no, do not misunderstand me. I have no embarrassment about my friendship with your father, or what was between us so long ago. My embarrassment was more for you, anticipating how difficult it must be to grasp something so abruptly and absorb it all. I'm a shy person and I sense a certain shyness in you, which makes me feel protective. I want you to be comfortable, but perhaps you cannot. I must have said something upsetting. You were smiling, but now there are lines of strain in your face. Here, let me get us some tea." She hurried off to the kitchen.

Glynnis felt foolish for being so heavy handed with someone who was not only kind and intelligent, but sensitive, as well. 'Am I so thick headed I don't remember all those powerful promises to myself? I'm hiding again. If I shrink back just enough, let my manner be just a wee bit haughty, we can complete this visit politely and I can leave quickly. Father's wishes will be respected, but I will remain untouched by it all. That's exactly what I would have done a week ago. But I will not let that happen. Father wanted to give me something. I marvel at the timing. I'm here, trying to learn a little self-reliance, and today Father's letter is delivered to me. Allison would tell me to lighten up, to enjoy this. Well, that's just what I'll do.' Glynnis got up and followed Alesa to the kitchen.

"Here, Alesa, let me help. Besides, I wanted to see your kitchen. I suspected it would be charming, and it is!"

"Ah, there is that marvelous smile again. You came back! For a little while I thought you were drifting away from me, from this. Here, let's take our tea outside." Alesa carried the red lacquered tea tray to the lanai.

"I want to talk about your father and share some memories so that you will know a little more about Eddie."

"Eddie?" Astonishment froze Glynnis in place. "You mean Father?" Her disbelieving look caused Alesa to throw back her head and laugh.

"Of course your father. My beach boy, Eddie! Oh, I know, on the mainland he was always Edward. But I think when he came to Honolulu he wanted to let his hair down a little since he was far from home. He forgot once and signed a letter to me 'Edward,' and I never let him forget how funny it sounded. I called him a stuffy old coot! To me he was always Eddie. In a funny way, because of that, I could separate him into two parts, my sweet, young Eddie and Edward, the wonderful husband and father and dignified businessman he was to you and the rest of the world. It was my secret, but an innocent secret. I don't believe it hurt anyone."

"No, Alesa, you're right. It didn't. But Eddie? I just can't imagine it. Not Father. He was so proper and, well, formal." As Glynnis paused, she saw the familiar picture of her father . . . three-piece suit of charcoal gray or black, conservative tie, trim gray hat, his carefully polished, elegant shoes. Dignified and proud. Gentle, but always reserved. A smile found its way to her face that quickly erupted into laughter. "I'm sorry. I'm not making fun of you or him. It's just that this thought came into my head of being with Father in his wonderful, quiet study just one time and Mother coming to the door, saying casually, 'Eddie, supper is ready.' I'm embarrassed to even think of such a thing, but I can't get it out of my mind!"

"Oh my, now, I can see that you are every bit as much a rascal as I am." Alesa's eyes twinkled gleefully.

"But you asked about the house. When I met your father I was renting the little apartment upstairs as a studio, and that's where we lived. When he left, I was going to move, but I just couldn't bear to leave all the memories behind. So I stayed on." Her head tilted upward toward the second floor. "Up there in the studio. A few years later the family that owned the place moved to Maui, and they sold this house to me. So you see, I'm just like that thorny kiave bush you see growing all over the Island. Once I get my roots down, you can't pry me out!"

The two settled down on the lanai, amidst rambunctious tropical vines that covered the walls of the sunny porch. Alesa brought out an old photograph album. The first pages were filled with snapshots of Father and Alesa, sometimes with Uncle John and Alesa's sister, Emma. Glynnis could see the happiness in every face, young people in love, and was comforted when she realized how exciting this time had been for Father.

"Now you can meet the rest of the family. There's lots of us to get to know." Alesa turned to pages full of pictures taken over the years. She pointed to a family photo taken on a beach. The bathing suit styles unquestionably placed the time of the photo at about forty years ago. "Here we are at Waimanalo beach. Can you find me?" She grinned as Glynnis studied the group.

"Oh, that must be you, next to the older lady. It is you, isn't it! You were beautiful. Well, what I mean is, you were beautiful then, as you are now!" Glynnis stammered, feeling foolish.

"I am a wrinkled old lady now! But I guess I was pretty

then. All young girls are pretty, you know. And the older lady next to me is my mother. She was so graceful and she was beautiful." Alesa was smiling at her mother's picture, lost in reflection.

"And the others? Who are they?" Glynnis' attention was drawn in particular to a young boy sitting in the sand next to Alesa's mother, a fair-haired, handsome youngster. "What a darling little boy. Is he a relative?"

"Oh, that's Timmy. Emma's boy." Alesa hesitated. "My sister Emma and John Halverson were married, you know." Glynnis nodded that she knew. "Dear Emma died when Timothy was born. Poor John was torn apart, of course, and he tried so hard to raise Tim. But in the end he knew it wasn't working for either of them. Mama and I told him that in our Hawaiian family Tim would be absorbed into our lives as though he were our very own—he *was* our very own. The spirit of ohana—family—is very strong in our lives, and often it happens that it is best for a child to be raised by another relative rather than the parents. He or she becomes their 'hanai' son or daughter, nurtured as their own. As Timmy grew up, it was hard to tell which one of us really acted as his mother, Mama or me. We swamped him with love and care. And of course our dear John has always remained a father to Timmy, coming to visit almost every year, taking part in decisions about his life, contributing to his upbringing. Not just financially, more important, guiding and teaching him. Yes, Emma would be happy, I know. He's a fine boy." Alesa wiped a tear from her eye.

"I just can't picture Uncle John as a father. And I certainly didn't think of him coming to Hawaii all the time. I do remember he liked the Islands for vacationing, but it seemed so casual. I never suspected. How hard it must have been—still must be—for him." Glynnis studied the picture, looking at the young boy, trying to see a likeness to the John Halverson she knew.

"It was hard. Losing Emma was hard. After that, it was just a matter of how to raise this wonderful child in the best way he could, without her. And I think it's worked out. Timothy is an angel. His mother would be so proud of him. There's nothing he can't do, so talented and clever. A hard worker, too. And he spoils me terribly. I love it!" Alesa laughed, and turned the page. "So let's continue, and you can follow us through the years."

They did just that, and Glynnis watched with special interest as the photos tracked young Timothy Halverson. She could see similarities between him and Uncle John growing more prominent as he grew older. Although of darker complexion and with some dissimilar features, the tall, sandy blonde haired figure was reminiscent of his father, and he looked into the camera with those same smiling eyes that captivated everyone who met Uncle John.

When they turned the last page of the album, Glynnis sighed. "What a warm and wonderful family you have, Alesa. Everyone is so happy. In each picture they're all smiles. And I don't think they're just posing. They are so warm and open. You all seem—natural, comfortable. You make me feel I've lived my life in a shell." Glynnis frowned as she felt familiar regrets pushing in around her happiness again.

"Don't be silly. You live in a different place, with a different set of rules. This is what I told your father so often. You're no different from me, don't you see? It's just that you'd look foolish cutting up in the middle of Philadelphia society, don't you think?" Alesa's laugh was tinged with sadness, and the younger woman knew she was talking more about herself than she was about her young visitor. This was part of what had forced her to give Father up and send him back where he needed to be, knowing she could not go with him, that she would not survive there, that they could not be happy.

They sat quietly for a while, pensive. As Glynnis gazed out over the housetops toward the sea far below, Alesa studied the woman she had always loved from afar. So wonderful it was to have her here at last, but it was a bittersweet meeting; the price of this day had been the passing of her loved one, Glynnis' father. Her Eddie. The years alone after he left had been bleak and painful at first, but she had overcome her desolation because it was her nature to be a sparkling, vivacious person. Her life had been touched, as all lives were, with tragedy and loss, yes, but, she reminded herself, weren't we all given the chance for a good life here on earth, and didn't we owe our family, friends and even ourselves something more than melancholy gloom? And now, imagine the kindness of Eddie, giving her one last touching gift, letting her know his treasured daughter, and sharing their story with her.

Glynnis studied the view, thinking of this marvelous woman and how they were tied to one another in a remarkable way. They had been isolated from each other by years, by thousands of miles and, most importantly, secrecy, yet there was an undeniable kinship, and an immediate affection that represented much more than the short time they'd known each other, in her case even known of the other's existence. Somewhere in the rich soup of instincts, genetic traits and learned habits, a link to Alesa had been formed long ago. Perhaps in things Father taught her, told her. An attitude, a tenderness. Whatever it was, she knew Alesa. Certainly it must have slipped through a crack in the carefully constructed traditional Philadelphia building blocks that cemented her upbringing. Had Alesa come into their home, Mother would have been polite, proper, but disapproving of someone so open and uninhibited. Mother would have called her "different," her speech "rather foreign" or "somewhat inappropriate." Glynnis blanched, realizing how taut and narrow her mother's standards were. And she recoiled from the realization that she had never questioned that somewhat arrogant social code. Alesa had been right not to expose herself to such attitudes. It was one thing to be born into that framework, as Mother had been. But Alesa's spirit would have crumpled under the austerity of emotion and gaiety.

The sound of a piano nudged its way into Glynnis' mind, at first subtle, but soon she was distinctly aware of the playing.

"That's Brahms. Someone's playing the Rhapsody Number Two. It's marvelous!" Glynnis listened intently, closing her eyes as she followed the music.

Alesa smiled. "That's Timmy. He must have gone upstairs without bothering us. That boy spends hours and hours at his piano. I've told him, if he loved to gamble as much as he loves his music, we'd all be wealthy. Or bankrupt!"

"How strange. I've loved that piece for so many years. In fact, at college I chose it for my Master's recital." Glynnis hesitated, listening. "Timothy understands the piece. He plays it wonderfully."

"We'll just have to get him down here so you can tell him yourself!" Alesa jumped up and walked to an intercom built into the wall. "Tim, come down, would you please? There's someone I want you to meet. You will be so surprised!" Her face was glowing with anticipation, Glynnis' frozen in panic.

There was shuffling overhead and then footsteps sounded on the stairway. Two well-tanned and muscular legs appeared, then a pair of faded swimming shorts, followed by the rest of a T-shirted man, bronzed by the sun, face and eyes smiling a welcome. The streaks of gray that tinged his sandy hair suggested he was in his forties, but there was a youthful vigor and graceful agility about him.

"Sorry, I was banging away upstairs and didn't know you had company. I'll keep it down." Smiling, he held Alesa affectionately by the shoulders and kissed her cheek.

"Now, I want you to meet my guest. You're not going to believe who has come to see me. Timothy, this is Glynnis Paxton. She came all the way from Philadelphia and just look, here she is in our home. Isn't this a miracle!" Alesa smiled. "Glynnis, I told you about our Timmy. Well, just look at him."

"Well, now I know why 'Lesa is laughing all over her face. I'm very happy to meet you, Glynnis. I've heard all about you from Dad." Timothy smiled warmly and took Glynnis' hand.

Incredible. This stranger greeting her and talking so casually about Uncle John as his 'Dad'. Nervously, Glynnis shook hands with the charming man. "I'm very pleased to meet you, too. It's a real honor." Honor! What a foolish thing to say. Her handshake was awkward and formal. Why was she acting like a jittery high school freshman who'd been called to the Principal's office? She chastised herself and frowned in anger at such ineptitude. *How stiff and proper can I be! Can't I act relaxed just this once?*

Timothy was warm and open. "You're on the difficult end of this meeting, aren't you." It didn't go unnoticed by Glynnis that he'd sensed her discomfort and was trying to help her relax. "We have always known about you. 'Lesa's told me about you, Dad has talked about you. Besides, we've always known <u>we</u> were here! I know that you didn't know. You've walked into new territory, and it's got to be odd. But don't let it get you. Alesa's such a dear, anyone could fall in love with her in a second, and I'll bet you already have. And if it's any help to you, I'm pretty easy to know, even though I'm another surprise package. You'll probably need a good twenty-four hours to just get used to all this. I know I would. But I'm glad to be able to meet you. Just make sure you stay long enough to feel right at home, so we can all get to know one another better. I can promise you Alesa is hoping you never go!"

"You are kind. And I really have felt so comfortable here all afternoon. It's just that when you came in—I mean, I was a little overwhelmed."

"Well, having that effect on a beautiful lady is better than going unnoticed, any day!" Timothy was laughing. "So, I'll be going, let you two girls get back to your woman-talk."

Alesa pulled on his arm. "Don't run off now, let Glynnis tell you what she was telling me. About your playing."

Glynnis knew embarrassment had turned her face a fiery crimson. She was an outsider, someone he barely knew about. She was just an interesting footnote in the story of Alesa's early romance. The comfortable affinity she had for Alesa ebbed into the background. It was impossible not to like the woman, and to feel at home. But this was different. Of course, this was Uncle John's son, and he was very cordial. Certainly very attractive.

Why, then, did her self-confidence evaporate into thin air to leave her stammering foolishly. She longed to be able to smile warmly and continue chatting, carefree and relaxed.

She thought of Susan's advice and worked to bring her Grace Kelly aura into play. But Grace was eluding her. Suddenly she realized there was nothing to get distressed over, she'd been asked to comment on something that was second nature to her, music. There were no doubts about her knowledge, no fear of sounding foolish. It was this man who was rattling her, tilting her so off balance. He was charming and good looking, at ease. But she wasn't being asked to comment on any of that. Only his music, and he deserved her praise. Glynnis drew a deep breath and began to relax. She was relieved that as she spoke, her heart stopped pounding and her voice grew in strength and animation.

"You play that Brahms with total understanding of the piece. It was faultless. It shows you have had a thorough training. But more than that, you feel the music. Uncle John—your father—told me that to have merit, one's playing has to marry training and discipline with a musical soul."

"That's funny, that's exactly what he told me!" Timothy sat down close to Glynnis and smiled with enthusiasm. "Looks like we've both had the same coach."

"How extraordinary!" Glynnis was startled. "Now that I remember, it was Uncle John who persuaded me to study the Rhapsody, encouraged me to use it for my Master's. And a continent away he had done the same with you! Amazing."

"I like that, I really do. The two of us with a musical link, and we didn't even realize it. We do now, though. Will you play it for me?" Timothy's voice was eager with anticipation.

Had Susan and Allison been hidden in the shadows of the room when the question was asked, they'd have anticipated a flustered Glynnis finding excuses why she couldn't perform for these strangers. But they didn't know anything about Glynnis' musical strength. They had never seen her in her element. In this arena she wasn't awkward or tentative. This was her territory. Her friends would have been surprised and pleased.

"Oh, no. Today that's your piece. I'll play some Chopin. But remember, it's been a while since I've touched a piano. All the time I've been on vacation, but even before. I haven't done much since Mother and then Father became ill. So you've had fair warning!" As Glynnis smiled she automatically massaged her fingers, limbering them to play.

Alesa led the way up the stairs, and as they climbed each step revealed more and more of the studio. It was a spacious room, furnished with large sofas laden with jewel-toned pillows like muted rubies, emeralds, amethysts. A three-part screen separated the sofas from the piano, the panels covered with the same striking tapa cloth that Father had placed in his package to her. Glynnis was sure the screen was part of the decorating he and Alesa had done so long ago. Ample light streamed through a skylight. She looked across the room from the top of the stairway and stared directly at a large portrait of Father. A vibrant, smiling youth, relaxed and tanned, but undeniably Father. Well, Eddie.

Timothy saw her studying the picture and was quick to make conversation. "You know that Alesa is a terrific artist, don't you? This was her studio until she decided she didn't like climbing the extra stairs every day. Besides, I think she wanted to find a place where she could get me out of her hair when I visit, so she lets me use it. I guess she did that portrait of your father a good number of years ago. He looks a lot younger than I am. Very handsome, though. It's not hard to see where you got your good looks."

Glynnis blushed, embarrassed but pleased by the compliment. And the moment of standing face to face with her Father's portrait had been softened and was now easily accepted. "Oh, yes, Father wrote about this portrait. I think he felt you flattered him, Alesa."

"No one was ever more beautiful." Alesa laughed. "Like a movie star."

"Oh, my! Here we go again." Glynnis smiled. "But I see the piano, and it's magnificent." She played some strong chords and intricate runs to get the feel of it. "Let me play the Fantaisie-Impromptu." She inhaled deeply, and after sitting quietly for a moment, letting the music flow through her body at a subconscious level, her fingers flew over the keys and the music poured forth. It was glorious to play again.

When she stopped, there was a long silence. Alesa jumped up to hug her. "I know that piece. "I'm Always Chasing Rainbows!" It was beautiful, Glynnis. She patted her shoulders affectionately.

"You nailed it!" Timothy beamed, and Glynnis could see he shared her moment of accomplishment, understood the excitement of bringing forth beautiful music. "And that business about being out of practice. That was just to catch us off guard. You've inspired me to work even harder. You get shadings that I just don't hear when I play." He stared directly into her eyes, and seemed riveted. "If you want to, come over every day and use the piano. If you're like me, a day without a piano is a lost day."

"Thank you, although I've never heard it referred to as 'nailing it' before!" Glynnis smiled. "I would like to come back and practice another time. But I wouldn't want to bother you for all the world. You must practice many hours a day yourself." The young woman tried to downplay her enthusiasm.

"No worry. I'm in the middle of working out a project right now, so I'm not able to get over here as often as I'd like. Been hearing about it from Alesa, as you might expect, so it would do me good to make a point of being here more. And I want to hear more of your music. We could even try some duets, if you'd like. I've got some great Rachmaninoff stuff. And Brahms." There was no question that Timothy wanted her to accept. "Besides, as wonderful as that would be, there's more to life than the piano. I can show you around the Islands a little, explain some of our Hawaiian history. I'd really like to show you what I love about this place while you're here."

"I'm not sure. My new friend and I are staying with a third friend, and I shouldn't spend too much time away. We've become a little like the Three Musketeers, pretty inseparable. I would like to see you both again. But there's no risk of me becoming a hanger-on here, you'll be happy to know!" Glynnis didn't want them to think she expected to be entertained, or that they had to look after her, now that she had introduced herself into their lives so abruptly. But she did want to see more of Alesa. And of course it was only proper to get to know Timothy so she could congratulate Uncle John on what a wonderful son he had. "And speaking of my friends, I really have to go. They will be worrying about me." There were protests, but Glynnis persuaded them of the need to leave. She hugged Alesa and they said their goodbyes, accompanied by happy tears and plans for another meeting soon. Timothy clasped her warmly with both arms, telling her to be prepared for a call very soon.

The taxi was turning into the condo driveway before a smiling Glynnis realized she'd ridden without a moment's hesitation clear across town with a cabbie who was totally unknown to her.

*Chapter Eight*

# Wednesday Evening

**A few minutes** later, when Susan and Allison saw their friend coming into the living room, they were bursting with curiosity, wanting to know what sudden business had taken Glynnis away so unexpectedly, and puzzled by her obvious exhilaration. For over an hour they listened, mesmerized, as her odyssey unfolded: the mystery letter revealing the remarkable, romantic tale of her father and Alesa, a haunting story of her family friend, John, suddenly widowed and left with an infant son. Then as Glynnis recounted her decision to visit Alesa and the events of the afternoon, Allison and Susan were on the edge of their chairs, fascinated and quite astonished. Glynnis told them of meeting Timothy, and described him.

"Sounds like a hunk!" Allison teased Glynnis. And you say he invited you back to use his piano? That's a new line!"

"Allison, you're dreadful! He's a musician and he recognizes that I miss my piano. He's also the son of my godfather, and he's trying to be a good host. That's all it is. You're just trying to embarrass me, but you won't succeed." Glynnis smiled, acknowledging to herself that she did feel strangely excited by the thought of the handsome Timothy.

They chose to go out for dinner to a restaurant at the end of Waikiki Beach. Susan reserved a table by the window overlooking the ocean. They enjoyed a more traditional dinner of rack of lamb that had been prepared exquisitely, surrounded by tiny roasted potatoes and julienned vegetables. The three sat admiring the view and Glynnis tried to picture this as the very beach where her father and Alesa found such happiness so many years ago. Many things must have changed, but the ocean was timeless. She reflected on how the disclosures of the day would affect her life and hoped in some way she would use this in the way her father wanted.

"My father gave me such a strange gift. I worry that I won't know how to use it," Glynnis looked across the table at the other two, her face showing concern.

"You're doing wonderfully, don't worry about anything. Hats off to you for absorbing all this in one day and hanging onto your perspective. With staggering news like that, you could have been buried by the fallout. Just stay the course, you'll be just fine." Susan smiled in admiration.

"If you think I'm managing it well enough, I'm pleased beyond all my expectations. However, I feel so weary—as though I've been working at hard labor all day. Would you mind if we made it an early night?" Glynnis suddenly could think of nothing better than a good night's sleep.

"You've earned it, girl, after a blockbuster day!" And by the way, my dear, what was all that about 'dull, unrelenting gray?' What I see before me is more like a radiant rainbow!" Allison patted her on the shoulder with a warm smile as the three finished and left.

Once home, Glynnis went directly to her room and to bed. Allison followed suit soon after, saying that she wanted some quiet time to think a bit before calling Joe in the morning.

"I know how you feel. I'm going to do a little soul searching, myself." Susan nodded in agreement. "Allison, I inherited my mother's knack for intuitive thinking, and something tells me things are going to work out between you and your husband. And I'm pulling for you, if that does any good at all."

"Hey, when something is stuck in the mud, a person needs all the friends they can find to push. I need all your good thoughts, and I thank you for wading in there to help." Allison waved and was off down the hall to bed.

Glynnis showered and climbed into bed, glowing with an inner warmth and exhilarated with happiness. She couldn't get Timothy Halverson out of her mind, remembering every detail of their meeting. At first she chided herself for such frivolous feelings and tried to account for his gentle interest as a politeness born of her relationship with his father, Uncle John. But she knew with deep conviction that this was not the reason. She closed her eyes and his image was vivid in her mind, and Glynnis was distracted and excited by the memory of him. She reached for the little book of poetry sent by her father and read until she fell asleep.

*So am I making any sense out of this mess yet?* Allison sat in a comfortable chair looking out over the palm trees toward the ocean. Through the open window the delightful scents of the tropical garden filled her bedroom. She had stopped by the kitchen and fixed a carafe of coffee and already had poured a large mug.

*I haven't gotten anywhere with Joe yet, but I'm going to get him to discuss it tomorrow. I know I can get him to open up and talk. And beyond that and until then, I really can't figure anything out. I have to know what he's thinking, what's going on. It won't do me any good to beat the situation to death with worry.*

*What gets me is that now that I've thought about it, it's not just the affair that has me troubled. All of a sudden I see things that aren't so good between us. I think I'd better just put a lid on it, though, until I've got more to work with. What was that story Dad used to read to me about Meddlesome Mattie, the little girl that couldn't keep her hands off things and usually ended up breaking or ruining them, and always got in trouble because of it. She blamed it on her hands. Seems like I'd better leave bad enough alone, keep hands off this mess, or I'll follow in Mattie's footsteps, sure as shooting. So, lady, the smart thing to do is finish this coffee and march off to bed so you'll be ready for tomorrow.*

Suddenly the house seemed unbearably quiet to Susan. She yearned for Allison or Glynnis to wander back into the living room so that she could visit with them instead of making this phone call to Philip. *It's strange. It wasn't hard to phone Mother and talk to her, but I'd give anything if I didn't have to make this call. On the other hand, not only must I tell Phil, I honestly want him to know. This is reality, and he has a right to be part of the picture. So without further delay . . .* Susan walked to the phone and dialed his number in San Francisco.

The line crackled and spit while Susan waited to hear Philip answer. When he did, she could barely understand his words because of interference.

"Philip, this is Susan. You sound like you're in a coal mine or something."

"Susan. I didn't expect to hear from you. Look, I'm in New York, having my calls forwarded from home, and that accounts for the bad connection. I'll call you right back. Are you at your folks' place in Kahala?"

"Yes, Phil. And thank you. I really can't imagine talking on this line. I'll wait for your call." Susan hung up and fidgeted with the phone cord and the watched the phone expectantly. When it rang, she jumped.

"Hello, Philip? I'm glad you're getting your calls forwarded because I really did want to talk to you tonight. I have some issues I need to go over with you. Are you free for a while?"

"Of course, Sue. I'm glad you got in touch. Are you feeling okay? You were pretty banged up when you left for Hawaii. I've been concerned about you. Whatever may have happened between us, you know I care."

Hearing the soft and grainy voice reminded Susan of their time together. It was so familiar, had been so much a part of her life and plans. When she fled to Hawaii, Susan thought she was putting Phil out of her life, but she could see now she'd never stopped loving this man, and whether she'd blown the relationship or not she always would. But this was more important than her feelings, and she brought herself up straight, knowing the emotional twists and turns would have to wait until she'd taken care of this all-important phone call.

"I'm feeling more relaxed, Phil. Thanks for asking. But this phone call is quite important, and I'd best get on with it. I arrived here in pretty bad shape, as you say. For want of a better description, I was a mess. But I thought the sun and relaxation would help, and I tried to unwind and start repairing." She hesitated, took a deep breath and went on.

"That's when I discovered that I'm pregnant. You'd think it would have occurred to me before, but I was too mentally bankrupt to think straight." She bit her lip, prepared to go on.

"Susan, I can't believe you're saying this. You're pregnant. My mind's going in every direction at once. I want to tell you

I'm the happiest man alive, but that's not really appropriate, is it? I mean, God, Sue, what does all this mean?" Philip's voice was urgent, pleading to hear the words he wanted Susan to say. Susan felt protective, he sounded so vulnerable, like a young boy.

"I've got to be honest with you, Phil. At first the only thing I could think about was having an abortion, but I soon realized I couldn't make that kind of choice so quickly. Then it hit me like a thunderbolt that you had a right to know, and to at least be aware of whatever my decision was."

Philip wanted to jump in, to urge Susan to reconsider. But how well he knew her. So he wisely said nothing, letting Susan complete her story.

"But dealing with the fact that I'm pregnant has required me to think about my whole life, my goals, dreams, and most importantly, about you." There was a moment of quiet, then she went on. "You know I love you, that's why it was so hard for me to end it between us, and I've been in pain ever since. The only obstruction for us was the baby thing. Now the whole issue has been thrown right into our lap.

"It's been hard examining my feelings about having a family, but I've tried to do it, and realize there was a lot of damage control going on which pushed me to the decision not to have children. Now I see I have been taking the easy way. Now that there's a real life started, and I am responsible for starting that life, I can't be so selfish anymore.

"So I've decided I want to keep this child. Before I called you I resolved that whatever I did, you shouldn't be bound in any way. I've hurt you far more than you deserve, and I would understand if I've burnt my bridges to our life together.

If that's true, and you've moved on to another phase of your life, if you've given up on me, I will do this by myself, and with no bad feelings. I just know I cannot put an end to this new life. I've come to realize how precious a gift it is, and I'm truly awed. And humbled. But I can do a good job of raising a child. I know I can." All at once her strength evaporated. There was a long silence on the line that chilled her. Only because she could hear the crackling of the long distance connection was she sure Philip was still on the line.

Susan was suddenly subdued and very vulnerable. "But what I want most in the world is to find out that you still care for me and we can be together. I guess that's what I need to say." Her voice was uncharacteristically small and anxious.

"I've got to be in New York a couple of days longer. Then I plan to get a plane and come over there and marry you, bring you home, and hopefully you'll learn to cook a little before this baby is walking." Philip was laughing, but he became serious.

"Sue, I was never angry about your decision. I was broken-hearted, but you did what you did because you were being honest. I argued my case as hard as I could, but when it didn't change your mind, I could only admire you for your integrity. I didn't feel that anything would ever be good again. I knew I'd have to go on and work with my life without the person I loved. That was the way it was going to have to be. But, honestly, I just couldn't imagine reversing gears and starting off in some new direction with somebody else. I liked "us," and I couldn't believe we wouldn't get another chance. So my life has pretty much been on hold, and therefore, lady, I can only say I'm happy you've come to your senses!" He laughed. "Can you imagine we're going to be parents? I'm still in shock."

Susan smiled. "I can imagine it, all right. And I still have doubts about how good a mother I'll be. But I think we'll have a strong enough baby to survive even a klutzy mother."

Her voice became quieter as she continued. "Philip, I am luckier than I deserve to be, and I don't really know how you're able to understand. I've never dealt with such a hang-up before. It made me clumsy and foolish, and without meaning to, I pushed my luck beyond the limit. I almost lost you, and I hurt you, besides.

"I really had no right to expect this outcome. Dad taught me an important lesson while I was learning to swim. He said if I would stay absolutely still in an upright position in the water, arms straight down, I would bob up and down, my nose just out of the water, so I could breathe. He told me I would never drown if I'd stay perfectly calm and quiet and trust what I knew. When we disagreed about having children I should have realized that I'd forgotten to apply Dad's lesson to that part of my life. I was flailing around like Daffy Duck. I should have just trusted what I knew, and especially I should have trusted you.

"I've learned a lot about myself that has finally let me work out of a mental block. But I repeat, I am incredibly lucky, and you are unbelievably good. I won't ever forget that, but if I should, remind me, all right? Because I love you even more than I did before, and I cannot wait for you to get here. I've missed you so, and wasted so much time. And there's everything to look forward to. I never thought life would be so good."

"Sue, if you wonder why I'm able to understand, it's because your father's lessons are true for all of us. I waited because I trusted my love for you and trusted you. You didn't let me down. I like your father a lot, and Peggy is a sweetheart. And they raised a pretty fine daughter who I happen to love. Incidentally, your mother told me not to count us out just yet, so I didn't." Philip waited for the reaction he knew that would bring.

"You two were scheming! I should have known." Susan was beaming. "But I'm so happy you were smart enough to listen to her. Now, how soon can you get here, Counselor?"

"I'll phone you as soon as I have my flight arranged. Can you arrange for someone to marry us, or do you want to wait until I get there?"

"We'll do it together. I like the sound of that. Hurry over here, please."

"I'll be there before you know it. Lord, Susan, you must have had one hell of a time with this. The good thing about it, though, is that making tough decisions is second nature to you. You always have been able to look logically at problems and work to a good resolution. So tell me, how did you work through this?"

She thought about how she could reply, then answered sheepishly, "Don't laugh. I had no plan, didn't know what I was going to do, until I heard your voice." Susan sounded embarrassed. "And even then, it could have gone either way. I just threw it to instinct."

"Oh, my God, you're not going to change your mind next time you hear my voice, are you?" Phil sounded more amused than worried, but there was a trace of anxiety in his words.

"Don't you forget, Phil, I'm pregnant, and I have the right to act flighty and giddy if I want to. The one thing I can promise you is that now you've proposed to me, you're not getting out of it, whatever you do. So don't try any cute lawyer tricks on me, like diminished capacity or something. Remember, I'm a pretty good lawyer, too, and I can think just as fast as you can." She smiled. "In fact, I'm thinking for two now!"

"I love you, Susan. You are going to be a marvelous Mrs. Alexander. See you in a matter of days."

Susan felt strong and healthy for the first time in months. *I guess instincts sometimes work better than logic. I didn't realize just how easy this was going to be.* She patted her stomach and went to bed.

## Chapter Nine

# Thursday

**The morning pace** was slow and leisurely, everyone taking time to stretch and absorb the early warmth of another perfect day. The women took coffee, bowls of delicate, poached guavas, and their new favorite morning treat, a platter of toasted and buttered Portuguese sweet bread onto the lanai, where they talked over plans and ideas.

Glynnis needed to call John Halverson and tell him about yesterday's extraordinary events, and she secretly hoped there would be an early phone call from Timothy. With newly discovered willpower she swept away persistent fear that he had simply acted cordially because of her relationship to his father and, indirectly, to Alesa. Glynnis' heart simply would not let her fears take over to rob her of this splendid feeling. But she made no mention of the hoped-for call to the others. It would be too humiliating if the call never came. *I know now that when you step out of your old, predictable ways too suddenly it feels a little like a rollercoaster ride,* Glynnis mused, sighing deeply. *Is this how most people feel, I wonder? Will I get used to it?*

Even though the temptation was great, Susan didn't mention her decision about the baby or about Philip, preferring to tell her parents first. *It'll have to wait until later, but surely they can see it in my face,* she thought, smiling even more broadly. Today would be busy. Most important, she'd make an appointment with Dr. Liu to tell him, and thank him for his help. And she needed to do some preliminary investigation into their wedding plans. All of a sudden she wanted to plan it all. But no, it really would be more fun to do it together with Philip. She would have to decide whether to try to get Mother and Father here for the ceremony. And then, of course, Philip might want to bring his family and friends. Or maybe it was better with just the two of them. More important, how was she going to prepare for this little baby? She needed a whole makeover from career woman to mom in less than nine months. Otherwise the poor child would be out of luck. Was it a boy or girl? How would they decide on a name? Her mind was working hard at solving problems and absorbing the magnitude this. She needed to sit down. *I tell you, anybody can deal with out of control clients, knotty legal issues and stern judges, but a baby! Who would have imagined I'd be turned into a blithering idiot by such an innocent thing.* She smiled as she realized how long she had denied herself a chance to loosen up and even be giddy. *I remember one of Mother's famous emotional speeches—'The world's greatest, most vital minds can be struck dumb by a child's simple question.' I think I was in the third grade when I asked her why I couldn't learn to spit like Bobby Baker could. I guess that's how Mother did such a good job of parenting, a good supply of witticisms and dramatic admonitions. I can do that!* Susan laughed and got back to planning her day in town.

Allison had no luck reaching Joe and decided to wait around the house to try in the afternoon. Standing beside the window, she looked out at the sparkling day and shrugged in mock dismay. "Well, since you ladies have such pressing business matters to deal with, I will take advantage of my uncomplicated state. Until further notice I will be extremely busy out in the sun. So far, I've managed to develop the beginning of a tan without burning. If I can get a little browner I'll be the envy of all my friends when I get back." She frowned and looked down, then recovered. "I mean, if I go back. Anyway, there's something almost wicked about sprawling out under a tropical sun and letting your skin turn golden. And I feel like indulging myself!"

Susan laughed. "If you really want to feel sinful, there's a small garden just off my bedroom, enclosed and absolutely private. Go on out there, strip off everything, and relax. It's instant gratification and the epitome of decadence. And no tan lines! Just remember to use plenty of sun block. If you get burned in those places that never see the sun, you'll pay dearly for your self-indulgence. Agonizing pain. Don't ask me how I know!"

Allison was all smiles. "I'm going for it! Hey, Glynnis, how about skinny-dipping in the sun with me? You can do your phoning later. Haven't you always wanted to be caressed sensuously by Mother Nature?"

Glynnis blushed bright crimson and quickly declined. "Oh, you know me. I'm embarrassed enough as it is just putting on that bikini I bought in Waikiki. I couldn't—well, I just couldn't." Nervous hands automatically moved to her throat and fussed to smooth and arrange her already neat collar.

"You know, as much as I want to change, it was definitely easier being the old, drab me. Back then, a significant moment in my day was helping Mother update her social calendar or analyzing some market reports for Father. Dull, certainly, but so much less complicated. And definitely not embarrassing, Allison!" She playfully wagged her finger at her friend, then paused. A look of surprise crossed her face as something occurred to her. "On the other hand ..." Her cheeks reddened again, and she lingered, seeming to waver between continuing the thought or stopping. At last she continued with a tentative voice. "It just occurred to me, though, that in my life music has been a very sensual, satisfying element. There is a passion, even if it exists in the mind, with only the piano to create a remarkable fulfillment. Now that I realize that, I do understand what it all means."

Allison was surprised. "Whoa, Glynny, all this philosophy just because I suggested some naked sunbathing? What's going on in your life that we don't know about, huh?"

"Don't be silly. And remember, naked sunbathing, as you put it, isn't really a thing I've talked about or considered ordinarily. You threw me off balance." To herself Glynnis realized she was thinking more of Timothy than of lying in the sun, and it must be showing.

"Well, anyway, if you won't come with me, then I'm off to bask." Allison danced down the hall. In the bedroom she peeled off her clothes, rummaged through her things and found a long sleepshirt to wear to and from the garden. The first night in Hawaii Allison had quickly realized that to wear anything to bed was to be too hot, and the T-shirt went back into her suitcase, unused. Laughing, she congratulated herself that all along she'd known there would be some use, that it hadn't taken up any of the meager space in the suitcase unnecessarily. *If nothing else had come up, I guess I'd have worn it shopping or something. But then I'd have had to explain to anyone who saw me that I don't usually wear clothing that proclaims "I'm Great!" except when it was proudly presented as a Mother's Day present by a very loving daughter. No, this is the perfect time for it. I'm off to pamper myself to death, and I'll announce my 'Greatness' right across my chest.*

Off came her watch, a threat to the goal of a seamless tan. As she pulled it over her hand, she noticed the wedding ring. Better take that off, too. Even a tiny line would spoil the total effect. But Allison resisted for a moment, not totally comfortable with the idea. Shaking her head as if to let loose cobwebs, she twisted it off her finger and laid it carefully on the table next to the watch. *For heaven's sake, you blockhead. There's no mystical importance to taking it off. You didn't say, 'I divorce thee' three times or anything. Cut out the drama and get on with the fabulous tan!*

The garden was beautiful, a fragrant statement in white. A pathway of chalky stones meandered through gardenia bushes and plumerias. Susan's lounge chair was situated just next to an arbor that supported a magnificent stephanotis vine. Throughout high school Allison worked summers in her father's florist shop and was familiar with that intoxicating flower with a scent so heavenly it was a favorite for bridal wreaths. "No wonder we girls get married. Everything about a wedding is simply gorgeous and we just get hypnotized into it. And you're profiting off our weaknesses by making up these irresistible bouquets," she had teased her dad one summer when she came home from college. Now she inhaled deeply, absorbing the romantic mood of the garden. The white blossoms of gardenias, plumerias and stephanotis competed with each other, flaunting their beauty against deep green leaves, each enticing you to linger with their sweet perfume.

Taking a quick look around to assure herself this place was as private as Susan promised, Allison pulled off her only garment and instantly felt the embrace of the warm sun.

*Oh, God, I'll never leave here!* Indeed, there was nothing

but peace and beauty and the tropical sun to indulge yourself. *Susan had to be insane to miss even one year coming here.* She
thought a moment and recalled how hard it is to shed responsibilities and routine even for pure pleasure. *Poor lady. It would
have done her good.*

Stretched out on the lounge, eyes closed, Allison attempted to stop the litany of problems from flooding her mind. The
chaos in her life seemed to trail behind her like a determined
shadow. *I can't get this stuff out of my head, not even for a moment,*
she complained to herself. *But I know there's going to come a time
when I can think it all through clearly. Like I've told the kids when
they bug me to decide something, I'm a strange bird. I've got all the
facts. Now it's just got to cook in my head for a while. Doesn't do any
good to go over and over it until it's been processed at some subconscious level. That's how my mind works, nutty as it is. Throw everything
in the hopper, let it work, and when it's been shaken and tossed around
enough, it'll be in a form I can work with. And I know it's not ready,
I'm not there yet. So as long as I'm enjoying a little bit of the lush life
this morning, come on, Lord, give me a little time.*

The sun caressed her, a secret lover, and finally her mind
and body flushed out every worrisome thought and concern.
She was a sponge, absorbing the pleasure, calm settling over
her like a warm blanket and lulling her to sleep.

Some time later she awoke, dreamily confused. Without a
watch she had no concept of the time. Funny, it didn't really
matter, this felt too marvelous. Allison examined her body,
relieved to see it was bright pink, but not burned. Wasn't it
remarkable how her skin, parched and old-looking from harsh
Alaskan weather, had become more supple and youthful in just
these few days under Hawaii's sky. *In a perfect world . . .* she

mused, imagining her beloved state with tropical breezes instead of the uncompromising dryness and cold that wreaked such havoc. *And if pigs could fly!* Laughing, she pulled the T-shirt on and reluctantly left the garden.

Entering the house, the sudden change from bright sun to the dimly lit hall made her dizzy and she squinted at the blackness. Instead of going directly to her bedroom she decided to go out into the front garden for a moment to adjust her eyes and head. Noticing Eric sitting at a lawn table under a stand of palms, she waved, remembering too late that she had nothing on except the crazy long T-shirt.

Eric returned her wave and called out. "I'm on a coffee break. Why don't you come over and help me finish off some of Noelani's cocoanut cookies. They're terrific."

*Great, now what have I gotten myself into?* But there was no choice except to go over. *Just walk slowly and you won't flounce all over the place,* she lectured herself.

"Hi, Eric. Quite a lizard life you have, sitting out here eating cookies and drinking coffee. I'll bet your days are just one long rest break!" During the short time she'd been there, Allison and Eric had hit it off very well. Since each had an active sense of humor and breezy honesty, they traded jabs and jokes with a comfortable friendliness.

"Maybe I've missed something, Miss 'I'm Great'," he teased, "but I can't remember you working up a sweat since you got here. Except for now, that is. You look pretty hot. But I'll bet it's not from hard labor, more likely lying in the sun. Exhausting work!"

Allison felt his eyes on her, thought he was looking with more interest than normal, a male hormonal interest, and couldn't decide if she liked it or not. *Hey, don't be a dummy. If a guy wants to notice me, I don't need special permission. Being married doesn't make me totally invisible. It's okay if somebody thinks I look attractive. He's not going to rape me, for heaven's sake. It's been a while since I felt anyone would check me out, so why not enjoy a little male attention. Anyway, it's only Eric. We're friends. He knows I'm married.* She paused. *I'm pretty sure he knows I'm married. I guess I've never said anything, but God, anyone would know that just from looking at me. I am the quintessential married woman. I could sit for the painting 'American Wife and Mother.' So what if seeing somebody get a little interested is kind of fun, that's a long day's hike from being the world's most notorious flirt! As a matter of fact, the very fact that being noticed surprises me says volumes. I feel like that old street dog in Homer—what's his name, Gomer—that's always begging for a bone or table scraps. God, girl, you are hard up for attention, aren't you!*

"Excuse me. Hello, Allison. Is anybody home? I think the sun has gotten to you. You're a thousand miles away. Can't a guy offer a pretty lady a cup of coffee around here?"

"Hey, my biggest problem right now is that I don't get this drinking hot coffee in the middle of a day when the temperature sits at a humid 79 degrees. I've been called weird by more than one person, but you don't see me doing something that crazy." She'd regained her balance and felt pretty relaxed.

"Well, I keep forgetting you're just a wrapped-in-bearskin Alaskan baby when it comes to the rugged, hard life we have to endure here in the tropics. Don't you know that drinking warm liquids is the best thing when the weather is hot?" Eric grinned at her.

*I'm feeling a lot more heat from sitting here almost stark naked than from the thought of any stupid cup of coffee,* Allison laughed to herself. *And until now I thought he was just a nice guy to joke around with. How come all of a sudden he's so damned good looking? This sun is getting to you, lady. Do something, fast!* "Hey, I'd better be getting indoors before I do get a burn. You're right, I really am a Northern wimp." She turned to go.

"Come on. I'll promise to stop teasing for at least five minutes if you'll give a lonely guy a break and at least share some of Lani's cookies with me. I'll even get you some lemonade, Miss Iceberg."

*Iceberg, huh? Is that what he thinks? Well, I can handle his little Hawaiian jab with a left to the jaw!* "What's with this 'Iceberg' stuff? You think I'm too cold and stuffy to deal with your Tropic of Cancer sense of humor?"

"Hold up there, darlin'. I meant it like, 'From Alaska,' you know. Like 'used to the cold weather, not used to the tropics.' Not like 'frigid,' if that's what you think. How could I say something like that about you? For one thing, I like you. I wouldn't hurt your feelings that way. For another, I've got a pretty good eye when it comes to ladies, and you're no iceberg. Sorry if I screwed up." He looked apologetic and bowed his head, then put his hand on top of hers and squeezed it. "Now please stay around and talk for awhile. And I'll go get you a lemonade."

"Well, I'll visit for a bit, but nix on the fruit juice. I'm going to swill down some of that hot coffee like I was born here. I'm tough—want to feel the sweat roll down my face, y'know! Isn't that what the tropics are all about?" Allison laughed and felt relaxed. She didn't know quite how to extricate her hand from under Eric's, but it seemed kind of comfortable and friendly of him, anyway, and she didn't want to hurt his feelings. *He is definitely a hunk!*

The two sipped coffee and laughed at each other's jokes for a half hour. When Eric looked at his watch he jumped up. "Oh, man, where'd the time go? I have to get back to work. But this has been great, Allison." He paused a moment, then plunged in. "You know, you're very pretty, and easy to talk to. Too bad for you to be here in the Islands with just girlfriends for company. It's such a damned romantic place. If I didn't think you already had a fella, I'd ask you out. But I suppose you do. Already have someone, I mean?" He looked cautiously hopeful.

*My God. I've been flirting with this guy and leading him on! What's gotten into me?* Allison sobered instantly and looked directly into his dark black, beautiful eyes, wavered, then continued. "You're right, Eric. I do already have someone. My husband. Sorry, I didn't mean to mislead you. I was just having a good time and, quite frankly, my ego needed some stroking, and your friendly attention did quite a good job of revving it up. Maybe a little too much, unfortunately. I don't make a habit of this, you know."

Eric patted her arm, then self-consciously pulled his hand back. "Well, you're a beautiful lady, and you've got something going on inside your head, more than what I call 'girl fluff.' Don't get offended, I just mean that sometimes women think a lot about themselves and how they look and all, and not a whole lot about anything else. You're different. You can't blame me for trying. I'd have been a fool not to. You've got a lucky husband. I'm sure he appreciates you, cause you deserve it."

*Like hell he appreciates me.* Allison stifled any comment, but reality hurt. "Well, thanks for the vote of approval. It was like getting drenched by the Fountain of Youth, and I needed that.

You're nice, too, and I had fun talking. You erased several wrin-kles from my face and slowed the onslaught of the first gray hairs, at least in my mind. Anyone who can do that gets my unending love and affection . . . well, friendship, anyway. And any time you're up Alaska way, drop in and I'll initiate you into our foreign but wonderful ways. That is, Joe, my husband, and I will." *That's right, just keep blithering on like a ninny. Why can't I end this conversation on a decent tone and get out of here? I've lost my senses.* Allison took a deep breath and tried to regain her composure. "I guess what I mean is, like they say in the movies, can't we still be friends?"

"Why shore 'nuff, ma'am." Eric beamed and tipped a non-ex-istent cowboy hat. "I'm mighty glad you didn't take no offense."

"I'm glad you aren't laughing at me. But I did learn an important thing."

"What's that?" Eric looked serious.

"Anybody who drinks coffee mid-day in Hawaii needs a touch-up on his supply of gray matter!" Allison smiled warm-ly. "Gotcha! Now, you'd better go or you'll be fired, and I've got to check that I don't have any second-degree burns on my back. See you soon, Eric." *God, he's gorgeous. Let me out of here before I do something I'll regret!* Allison clutched her towel to her and hurried off to the house.

Safely back in her room she took an unusually long time showering and dressing, feeling very much a woman of mys-tery and glamour. *I could be really embarrassed about the last hour, but I haven't felt this good in a long time, and I'm not going to ruin it by getting all clucky and virginal. It did me a world of good to be hit on, old lady that I am. And nothing happened, so I won't even have to wake up tomorrow morning hating myself. Kind of wish it had, though.*

*Do you hear that, Joe? You'd damn well better come to the party and get this whole thing ironed out because I think I'm wearing thin.* She swallowed hard and was immediately sobered.

Allison picked up the phone and dialed home. As it rang, she panicked at the thought of talking to Joe when the giddiness of the afternoon still clung to her thoughts. But then she heard his voice and it was too late to hang up or back out.

"Hello, Joe."

"Hi, Sonny. This is a pretty strange time to call. I was just on the way out to check on some repairs." He sounded a little rushed, irritated, even.

"I'm sorry to interrupt your busy schedule, Joe, but we've let this go way too long. We need to talk, and it's just got to be now. I need to hear from you just what is going on."

Joe's obstinate silence did battle against his wife's determination, and he might have outlasted her, but she suddenly lost patience and shouted into the phone.

"I don't have to wait for your admission, thank you very much. There's more than enough going on to convince me, and your refusal to talk about it just adds a final cruel touch. I thought you'd have the good manners and guts to at least come clean. But I suppose I'll learn that nothing's the same. Can't depend on the way things were anymore. And that ain't pretty, but I'll handle it. I certainly wouldn't want to upset your wildly romantic escapades for long enough to deal with the dreary details of your old life—me, our kids. Responsibilities can be such a bore, can't they! Even just explaining that you are having an affair is a lot to ask. It cuts into your precious time being a burgeoning stud."

It was good to get it out, and Allison could feel tensed muscles easing their grip. Even now it seemed he wasn't going to dignify her feelings with an explanation. The telephone felt heavy in her hand as the momentary triumph of telling him off drained away and a dull hollowness replaced it.

Allison heard him breathe, and had to strain to hear his words. "There's no affair, Sonny. Never has been."

She'd already inhaled deeply, ready to let fly at him, no matter how he answered. Instead, his words hit her full force and she hung suspended, mouth open, ready to speak, but with no idea how to respond, not even remembering to exhale.

She'd been so certain. But even if his refusal to talk about it, let alone apologize, were out of character, Joe would not lie to her. She would bet her life on that, despite the level of anger she felt. Joe was telling the truth. Slowly the breath that would have hurled her angry words at him carried them softly away, unspoken. She shook her head to clear aside the confusion and tried to formulate a reply. But it wasn't necessary.

Joe's voice was quiet but steady. "I don't know how things got away from me like this. But you're sure putting the pressure on." His voice rose with a tinge of antagonism. "Goddam it, I don't know how the hell to explain."

She bristled. "Joe, let me put it this way. It may be hard to explain, but you've definitely got my attention, so try, okay? I suggest you start from some kind of beginning and go from there to more or less where we are now. And by the way, I'm going to take custody of all the 'hells' and 'goddams.' I think I deserve them more than you do."

"Okay, okay, I hear you. This is just about as much fun as falling into a glacial lake. I guess the best way is to just dive in and get it over with." Joe's self-pity comforted him a little, but he was still under attack, and he knew it.

"Okay." He breathed deeply. "Well, I guess things started when I went in for my physical. You know how I hate doctors, always think they're going to find something horrible. Well, there was something in one of the tests that puzzled the doc, and he had me go down for some more tests. When I went into the lab I found that Rachel Morales, an old high school friend, worked there. While I was waiting for the results I took Rachel over to the cafeteria for a cup of coffee during her break, and we talked about old times, mutual friends, I told her all about you, and she showed me pictures of her husband and kids. I was pretty nervous about the lab tests and what they'd discover was wrong with me, thought it might be cancer or something, and I suppose I let her know how worried I was about the lab tests, and that's why she called the house after I'd gotten home. To make sure everything was all right. Of course by then, I'd already heard from Doc Blake and knew everything was okay. I swear, that's the truth. So now do you understand?"

"Not one little bit, Joe. Oh, I can see how the misunderstanding about this Rachel happened, and yes, I believe you. I know you, and you never learned how to lie. But none of this explains your attitude toward me. You've been distant, surly, might just as well be telling me you were tired of me. What goes, Joe, because this hits right at the heart of our marriage."

"I should have known you wouldn't let it go at that, that you'd want to go deeper. Don't know how to explain it, Sonny. You haven't done anything wrong. I guess everything in my life feels stale right now. It's probably hard for you to get it, because I know how happy you are. Everything you ever wanted has come true for you . . . the kids, a good home, . . ." He paused, embarrassed. "You've told me you're crazy about me. Well, for me, it's not that you're not great, and I love the kids, the business is starting to really come around. But I feel like there's something missing. Try to understand."

*Don't blow up at him or you'll never be able to fix it if you do,* Allison's grave admonition to herself was bitterly true and she knew it, so she paused before answering.

"When I said I'd marry you, I gave up a chance to pursue my own writing career. You may remember a couple of my English professors thought I had some talent. They gave me letters of introduction to various agents and editors they knew, and I had some big dreams going. But I loved you more than that.

"When I left Seattle and all my family and friends behind to go off to Alaska with you, it was a pretty tough thing to do. I still miss all of that. But I loved you, and figured it was worth it.

"Through the years we've been married I've had times when I wished you'd take a little time away from the everyday and surprise me with a little romance. Like you used to when we were dating. But you just seemed set on living the life you told me you wanted—a flying business in Homer, the small-town Alaskan life, surrounded by your childhood friends and your family. No worry about dressing up much or going anywhere exciting. But I loved you, Joe, and I loved our life, even without some of the things I hoped for. To put it mildly, I think this show of boredom with the life you chose yourself is a little inappropriate, not to say self-centered. Do you really think you're the only one who would like to inject some romance and luxury into their lives to stir up a little excitement?

"Seems to me your male menopause, or whatever the hell it is, has opened up a Pandora's box, because now we're both talking about the things we don't have, and how there's—how did you put it? There's something missing. Anyway, at least we've made headway in this discussion. Your head won't grow much bigger than it has, because—ta da!—you've learned you're not alone, Mr. Wonderful. I've sacrificed, too, and now that you mention it, there is something missing."

A voice in her head spoke to her. *Hold back, Allison my girl. You're getting into deep water.* She tried to rein in her anger.

"Look, Joe, I'm pretty blown away by what you've said. I'm probably not handling this too well right now. I'm going to hang up and call again later, after I've had time to digest everything."

"You're mad. I knew you'd be." Joe's answer almost made Allison laugh, it was so childish. But she was too hurt and disoriented to fully appreciate the humor.

"I've got to go, Joe. I'll call you." And she hung up. It was going to be a long day.

Timothy called early, relieving Glynnis of painful waiting. Within the hour he was at the front door, all smiles. "Alesa was up before dawn this morning preparing a lunch for you. She's already made every special dish she knows, some I've never even heard of. I told her not to tire herself out, and she just smiled. You've made her so happy. Speaking as someone who cherishes her, it's good to see her so cheery. Her life hasn't always been easy, yet she's always wanted to look after all of us that she cares about, and she deserves the very best." His face radiated happiness. "And you are that, to be sure."

Glynnis smiled and looked down. Life was idyllic and beautiful. She wore deep green slacks topped with a foam green and white print blouse. White shell earrings, bracelet and sandals, all recent purchases in Waikiki, completed her outfit. It pleased her that Timothy noticed, teasing that a for a Pennsylvania girl she looked pretty comfortable with Island wear. She smiled at how happy such a casual remark made her.

"Before we leave I want you to meet my friends. Susan is in the front room and Allison . . ." The vision of Allison skinny-dipping in the sun, as she called it, caught Glynnis mid-sentence. "Oh my, Allison isn't available right now, but there'll be other chances to meet her."

Susan was listening to music as she wrote out a list of errands, and smiled as Glynnis walked in with Timothy. So this was the cause of her friend's special glow. *Things in this household are improving at the speed of light. This girl has been a blossom waiting to open and she's finally discovered how to unfurl. So much goodness and quality inside, and just didn't know how to let it out. But I do believe she's caught on a little in the last few days. She radiates happiness. But I must admit that if it weren't for the unusual circumstances when we landed, I'd have walked right by, never notic-ing her.* She knew that if Glynnis had been a prospective juror or client, she'd have scribbled "mousy" by her name, indel-ibly tagging her with certain characteristics and habits that would follow her throughout their dealings with each other. *How wrong I would have been! That girl has shown a lot of courage and spirit. Now if only life will improve for Allison, we'll have what Mother would call a party begging to happen. With three guests of honor, imagine that!*

A proud Glynnis introduced Timothy to Susan and they

chatted against a background of Hawaiian music playing on the CD.

"You like that group, the Pandanus Club, too? They're favorites of mine." Timothy turned to Glynnis. "Don't know if you've had much opportunity to hear a lot of our local musicians, but there's some beautiful and authentic music that you should hear. They've learned the old language, and by using it in their music, they help carry on our traditions."

"Well, one night we listened to Susan's recording of slack key guitar, and I liked it very much. I guess we've been pretty busy, though, and haven't spent too much time relaxing. I'd love to hear more. It adds even more to the romance of being here! Not that I can understand anything they're saying, of course."

"A lot of the time they're singing about places they love. Our love for our land is very strong, and there's no embarrassment about saying so. Most of us will sing anywhere, anytime.

"In fact, I know a place you'd love, and we'll make a point of going there. All of us, you, Susan and your friend Allison. It's a restaurant at a small golf club. They have good food and a great piano player, but the best part is that everyone who's there sings, dances, whatever they want. Sometimes popular music, some '40s and '50s "Golden Oldies," but mostly, and to me the most phenomenal, performing our own Hawaiian music. We'll take Alesa, too, and everyone will have the chance to meet one another."

"Sounds fine to me. Just let us know when, Timothy." Susan looked at her watch. "But you'll have to excuse me, I've got a million errands to run in town, and the day is creeping away from me."

"If we don't get to Alesa's she'll have my hide. So we're on our way, too." Timothy put his hand on Glynnis' arm. "Are you ready, Chopin?"

"Oh, heavens." Glynnis blushed. "Yes, I'm ready. I don't want to keep Alesa waiting, and I can hardly wait to taste all the good things she's prepared."

"Then let's go!" Timothy steered her out to his car, a gleaming bright red Mustang, obviously a classic.

"What a beautiful old car. You must spend a lot of time polishing, it's absolutely glowing! What year is it?"

"The best, an original '65. Yep, I do some babying. You know, here in the Islands the weather rusts out even a new car pretty quickly, so it takes a lot of effort to keep this one in good shape." He opened the driver's door. "Want to drive?"

"Heavens no! My, you are a reckless individual, aren't you! I've seen the traffic and narrow streets, and I'd have us in an accident before we got out of the driveway." Glynnis didn't know whether to be terrified at the thought of driving or complimented that he'd trusted her enough to suggest it.

"We'll have you driving it in no time. Maybe on the way home." He opened the passenger door and helped her in. "Well, time's a'wasting. Better we go before Alesa has one big fit and it'll be pau for us."

As well spoken as he was, occasionally a little Hawaiian pidgen English surfaced in his speech, and it delighted Allison. "Whatever do you mean, 'pow,' that Alesa's going to hit us?" she laughed.

"No, 'pau,' like it'll be all over. It means to be finished. At five o'clock you leave work because you're pau. When you've eaten all you can eat, you're pau. Make sense?"

"Got it. So when I get pau with my lunch I will probably have gained 15 pounds," Allison said it a little stiffly, giggling.

"Now you've got it!"

When they arrived the air was filled with a mix of delicious aromas, and Alesa hugged her happily. Her muu-muu was as deep blue as the ocean, again trimmed with sparkling white lace. It was a joy to be in this friendly home again with the charming woman that Glynnis felt genuine affection for.

"I understand you've gone to a great deal of trouble to prepare this lunch, Alesa. I should scold you."

"No, don't be angry at me for doing what I love to do. I want you to enjoy some of our favorite things. Oh, if I'd had more time we'd have had a luau, a feast, but some of those dishes take days to prepare. But if you stay long enough we will do just that, and we'll dig an imu, and do kalua pig and everything. This is only a sampling, but I think you'll like it."

Timothy became the interpreter. "An imu is a pit that's lined with lava rock and wet kiave wood and food is buried and smoked and steamed for hours. The kalua pig is a whole pig that's wrapped and roasted until it's so well done it just falls into shreds, the most important part of a luau, but fish and chickens and yams are put in, too, and the taste is unforgettable."

Glynnis bit her lip nervously. "I'm not too adventurous when it comes to food. Maybe I would find the luau a little— exotic." *And this lunch, too, for all I know,* she worried.

"Trust me, darling, I wouldn't let you try anything too strange." Alesa smiled knowingly. For instance, some of us love sea urchins and such, but even Timmy says that's going too far." Glynnis shuddered, causing Alesa to laugh. "I will tell you what's in any dish that worries you, and if you don't want to try it, that's fine. I understand. There's plenty of things that are 'just food,' and only a few that might cause you a problem. You'll see! And speaking of all this food, we should eat. Come onto the lanai."

They moved onto the lanai where Glynnis saw a huge array of food on the table. She also noticed a dozen bouquets around the room. At least two dozen stems of gardenias crowded one vase.

"Everything looks beautiful, Alesa. The food, the flowers. I feel very special."

"Well, you are special, my dear, but these things are just the gifts we are given to use and enjoy. Nature's bounty. I picked the flowers in the garden this morning and by tomorrow morning there'll be just as many in their place."

Lunch was served, and Glynnis found almost every item unforgettably delicious. She asked about everything, and between Alesa and Timothy they gave her a gourmet's guide through the meal.

"Maui Onion Salad, there's no better onion on the face of the earth. So sweet." . . . "Ono, you probably know it as wahoo, a kind of mackerel. It's so good, we use the word 'ono' to mean delicious. This is prepared with macadamia nut sauce." . . . "Of course we have to have some of our teriyaki chicken. No Island meal is complete without that!" . . . "I tried to serve only vegetables that were locally grown—Waimanalo corn, melons from the butcher's own garden, papaya, these tiny sugar bananas, our local sweet potatoes, Manoa lettuce, avocados." . . . "This is manapua, it's a Chinese favorite. Just steamed dumplings with pork inside. Good, no? It was so sweet of Mr. Chan to bring them over."

And Timothy's encouraging words, "Now this is laulau, and there's nothing more delicious. It's pork and salted fish with our local spinach all wrapped in ti leaves and steamed. I see your expression, but just try it. For me! See, I knew you'd like it." He was beaming with such pleasure that Glynnis was glad she'd tried it, because she'd been about to decline.

"Now, this is a bit of a gamble. Tako poki. It's pickled seaweed with octopus." Glynnis' eyes grew very large. "Well, you can pass on that one till next time. But I warn you, it's so good, it's one of my favorites. Want to try a bite?" It was worth the difficulty swallowing to see his face shine with delight as Glynnis forced a taste. *It may take some time for that to be one of my favorites.* She shivered involuntarily, hoping no one would notice.

"We have only two desserts today, haupia, which is cocoanut pudding. My dear friend Eleanor Pahoa brought this over when she heard you were coming. And this is just simple vanilla ice cream with lilikoi—that's passion fruit. They're picked from the vine that you see as you come up the stairs. Remember the beautiful purple and green flowers. That's the one." Glynnis found both dishes delicious, but she was most intrigued by the strange, but unusual taste and appearance of the passion fruit.

"I don't think I'll eat again for the rest of my trip. Alesa, you prepared a feast fit for a queen. I'm going to write everything down in my journal when I get home so I won't forget any of these glorious dishes. Do you mind if I call you if I need help with names or ingredients?"

"You darling girl." A tear came to Alesa's eye. "When I think of all the good fortune I've been given in my life, and now to have this added gift. That tomorrow you might call me just to talk over a recipe, so simple and yet so meaningful—I don't deserve such happiness."

Timothy smiled as Glynnis answered. "I've found something so very valuable that I didn't even know existed. I didn't do anything to earn it, and probably don't deserve it. But your coming into my life has enriched it beyond measure, Alesa." She saw that the older woman was starting to cry. What would Allison say right now to lighten things up, she wondered, then chided, "Anyway, if I didn't say something nice, Timothy here would be after me, because he is your Number One fan. I can't have him angry with me!"

They laughed and visited awhile longer, and when they prepared to leave, Alesa protested.

"I want to take this lady on a grand tour of the city, Alesa, so I can watch her fall in love with it." Timothy hesitated and then suggested, "Of course you're welcome to come along."

The older woman smiled knowingly. "No, you know how tired I get in the afternoon. I need my nap. You young children go ahead." And they left, but only after Alesa had extracted the promise of a return visit.

Glynnis enjoyed their drive through downtown Honolulu, listening to Timothy's descriptions of its history, eccentricities, his favorite places, personal memories. He drove down North Market to the area known as Chinatown, pointing out where you could buy wonderful Asian delicacies, some that sounded quite astonishing. They drove past Iolani Palace and the statue of King Kamehameha. Glynnis was fascinated by the blend of old, modern, Eastern and Western cultures, traditional elegance and tawdry tourist spots.

"It's an exciting city. No wonder you love it. Certainly

not like Philadelphia! Well, some of it is. We have old, impressive buildings, too. But no Kamehameha! Just statues of the Founding Fathers and all that!"

"Well, all statues look a little pompous, don't they? But we admire and love them, anyway." He pointed to the statue. "One thing he can boast that I don't believe Ben Franklin or the others can is that on Kamehameha Day, this statue is draped with beautiful 18-foot flower leis. The people show their love to him, as they would their friends and family." Timothy's voice was warm with the gentle and genuine regard the people of the Islands have for one another.

"It's a wonderful way to show caring. I love it. When I first arrived a few days ago I was quite upset and lonely, until I met my friend, Allison. One of the first things she did was to purchase a lei and put it around my neck, with a kiss and welcome. That has to be one of the most touching gestures anyone has ever made to me, one I will never forget. I've realized ever since how deeply devoted people here are to one another. Quite a contrast to my hometown. Of course, Philadelphians are good people, but they most definitely don't show much emotion in public. Alesa said she chided Father once and called him 'stuffy,' and I suppose that's accurate. People there aren't mean spirited, just more distant, perhaps distrustful. It's what I grew up with, though, I'm used to it. But what a sharp contrast to the attitudes here. Everyone is so open, so willing to express their feelings, to show they care about you. Alesa's like that, you are, too. I'm a little envious!" Glynnis thought she sounded too serious speaking her views, but this was something that had impressed her, and she wanted to say it.

"Well, I'd hate to live anywhere else, that's true. Even

though I enjoy traveling, I can't explain it, there's something about Hawaii that makes it close to impossible to stay away too long. While I was growing up I spent lots of time during summer vacations on the mainland, going places with Dad. He always made sure I spent a week or so with friends in Southern California. They had a home right on the beach. I dreaded that time, not that they weren't great people, but whenever I went down to that beach and looked out at the Pacific Ocean, I'd remember that just over the horizon was my home, and it made me so homesick. Years later I told my father that, and he laughed, saying he planned that stay because he felt it would be nice for me to be in a familiar setting, on the beach, you know. Little did he know it darned near broke my heart every time.

"There's just something about this place. Everywhere I've traveled the people are wonderful, it's just that here they don't mind laying their feelings out in the open. They say it's the beautiful scenery and warm weather that keep you here, but I know it's the people. So watch out, if you get to like us too much, you might never go home!" Timothy's eyes were lively with fun as he spoke. "Of course, the beaches aren't bad, either.

"And you know, this tradition of giving leis—lots of people who visit us think that it's done as a tourist gimmick, but giving leis is a part of our life. Whatever the occasion, friends remember you with a lei. In fact, sometimes we just give them to show friendship. Every Friday is "Aloha Friday," and we give leis to friends at work, family, those we care about. And I'll tell you a secret. My favorite lei is plumeria. Know why? Because as old as I am, every time I smell a plumeria blossom I remember playing as a little keiki in my tutu's garden. I'm giving you another lesson in Hawaiian! Keiki means child and tutu is grandmother. My tutu—Alesa's mother—had a large back yard with five or six big plumeria trees. I just can't catch a whiff of that scent without being right back in her garden. And you never tire of it. But that's enough of that."

Glynnis studied her escort and was touched by his gentle nature. She marveled that he could be so sensitive yet at once very masculine. No one would laugh at his honest love of Hawaii. Somehow the spirit of this country embraced the strong, manly qualities, but left room for a tenderness not usually found in men. Glynnis was intrigued with this Timothy Halverson.

As they drove, he turned and asked with enthusiasm, "If you have a little extra time, I'd like to take you past my project. It's not very far out of the way. Want to see it?"

Glynnis couldn't resist his enthusiasm. "I'd like to. Just what is this project? I don't think you even told me what you do." Glynnis was intrigued.

"I have a small property management company. We handle vacation condos and rental homes all over the Island. When I was a kid I worked summers for a construction company and not only learned a lot about building, but I discovered I enjoyed working with houses and building sites, creating or maintaining something attractive and useful. So when I finished school I worked for a real estate company that had a property management unit to get experience, then went out on my own. I represent owners and handle the renting of their units, but also I've slowly bought properties that I thought were good investments.

"Recently I came upon a wonderful old mansion that was

being sold as part of an estate. Vacant for a long time and badly run down, but I fell in love with her instantly. The price was stiff for me, although for that area, and for the gem that she is, it was a steal. So I gritted my teeth and took a real gamble. Bought the place and now I'm renovating, giving that grand lady back her dignity. Doing most of the work myself. When I finish, I want to make it a Bed and Breakfast Inn. It's been a passion of mine to have an inn that was unusual, kind of my dream home, I guess. The place where I'd love to live myself—if I could afford to have a place with ten bedrooms." Timothy's voice was full of energy as he described his undertaking.

"Oh, I'd love to see it! It sounds remarkable. We'll make time." It wasn't hard to be caught up in the excitement.

Timothy turned the car toward the mountains and they headed up a broad highway lined with large homes. He told Glynnis this was the Pali Highway, and the mountains were the Koolaus ("Just think of 'oh-oh,' when you pronounce it—Kóh-oh-lauz. We'll have you speaking right in no time!"). Following to the top would bring them to the famed Pali Lookout, he explained, but they would save that for another day. When they'd traveled a short distance he veered to the right, explaining they were leaving the main highway for what was called the Old Pali Highway. "Used to be the main road, but now it's just a side road for the residents and for tourists who want to catch some beautiful scenery. This is where my place is."

The road wound through dense, old foliage. Trees overhung it from both sides, forming a canopy. Vines crept up the huge trunks and through the branches, some bearing flowers, others masses of green leaves. Glynnis noticed many homes, most old and gracious, but some were newer, built with less consideration for the ancient surroundings. She silently hoped that Timothy's property wouldn't be one of the newer, more garish ones. But then, it wouldn't suit his personality to be so inspired by anything less than a classic, she was certain.

"We're coming right up to it, just around that corner where you see the liana vines hanging so low." There was delight in the man's voice, obviously anxious to show off his prize. He pulled into a long driveway bordered by old, moss-covered rocks. "Here. Here it is. What do you think?" Although the seemingly limitless garden was overgrown and neglected, its basic artistic design showed through. "The jungle takes over pretty fast around here, but these old trees have been left to grow more and more beautiful. They just need some vines pulled away to give them more air and sunlight, some room to breathe. I've found wonderful plants of all kinds, so many varieties of hibiscus you'd be amazed. They need some tender loving care, but they're healthy." Timothy paused and smiled. "And then of course, there's the house."

"It's breathtaking. Look at all the porches—no, I mean lanais." Glynnis laughed. "You see, I've been paying attention and learning some Hawaiian words! These lanais are so wide and inviting. And windows everywhere. I can't believe the beautiful design. I think some member of royalty must have lived here, don't you? It's too glorious to be just a house."

"Oh, it's 'just a house,' no ghosts of kings or queens hidden in the closets. But it's a beauty, isn't it? Hey, you haven't said anything about the broken shutters on the windows, or the dismal paint job. She's glorious, but her beauty is a bit faded. She's showing her age." Glynnis could see that Timothy spoke the words honestly, but that he, too, was looking beyond the defects at the inherent beauty.

"Well, Mr. Halverson, I'd say you've found yourself a treasure. Like anything worth having, you have to look deeper than just surface wear and tear." As soon as she'd uttered the sentence, Glynnis flinched, her high spirits on the verge of plummeting. She had taken for granted he would use his father's name. Perhaps that was foolish. How could she be so brash. Maybe it was a very sensitive issue with him, and he'd be upset or even angry at the assumption. Happily, her worries were short-lived.

"I believe you're right, Miss Paxton. Mr. Halverson is a very lucky man." He hesitated, then smiled directly at her. "Right now, I'd say, more lucky than ever before."

Glynnis blushed, embarrassed.

They toured the house, and then sat on the lanai on a couple of old cane chairs. Looking out over the majestic grounds, the two visualized how it would be.

"That large hall will be a common area for the guests. There will be sofas and comfortable chairs. Walls of bookcases with all types of reading materials—histories, books on local plants and animals, atlases. Works about Hawaii and just casual reading stuff, too. People will be able to satisfy whatever mood they're in. Tables set up with chessboards, jigsaw puzzles, decks of cards and writing materials. I'll add Hawaiian artifacts as I can afford them. Alesa said she'd advise me on interior decoration. Naturally, being an artist she has a marvelous eye for that sort of thing."

They were brimming with ideas. Timothy described his plan for an outdoor hot tub sheltered by vine-covered trellises, the perfect place to relax with a tropical drink in the evening. Glynnis spoke excitedly about the breakfasts that could be served from the large, old-fashioned kitchen. Tables would be set up in the big dining room, on the lanai, and even some under the trees in the garden. And the delicious aromas of sweet breads and Island delicacies baking would draw throngs of guests.

"And a piano, of course." Glynnis beamed. "A piano and plenty of music. In the big room."

"Definitely a piano. It's funny you mentioned that. I had dreamed of offering one of the rooms as a grant to music students at the Academy. They'd be artists-in-residence here while they studied. Live rent-free. Trouble is, I can't afford anything like that. I'm just a hard-working businessman. I feel lucky enough to be able to incorporate this project into my work and justify it. So I'll wait until I've made my fortune to become a Patron of the Arts! But in the meantime, a piano I can swing." Timothy looked happily at Glynnis. "So you don't think this is a hare-brained idea?"

"In no way. You're going to have a huge success on your hands. I just know it." Glynnis enjoyed sharing his plans and dreams.

She glanced at her watch. "But now I really must get home. My friends will have the police out looking for me if I don't let them know I'm still alive and well."

They walked back along a path to the car through the overgrown garden, stopping under a large kukui tree to admire the property, visualizing it as it would be when the work was done. Glynnis sighed, pleased that her friend could fulfill his dream. Timothy turned to look at her, touched at her obvious enthusiasm for his plan. He held her gently by the shoulders, turned her toward him and kissed her.

Glynnis was startled, caught completely off guard, but surprisingly, not uncomfortable. Rather, she felt a wonderful dreamy pleasure. She closed her eyes for long seconds, then looked at Timothy with wide eyes.

"Please don't misunderstand me, I wasn't trying to—it's just that the moment came and I couldn't do anything but go along. I shouldn't have presumed . . ." Timothy hesitated, then laughed warmly. "Well, you said we Hawaiians were friendly. Also, it's obvious what good taste I have! You've seen this property and seem to approve, so you know I have a discerning eye! How could I not be attracted to a beautiful woman." His face grew more serious. "I hope I haven't offended."

Glynnis could feel her lip trembling. She was completely surprised, left without any idea what to say. Then, remembering his comment earlier that afternoon, she smiled. "Well, having such an effect on a handsome man is better than going unnoticed, any day!" She suddenly felt beautiful and infinitely happy as never before. A thought came to her. *Thanks, Allison, for showing my how helpful laughter and humor are.*

The two slowly walked back to the car and Timothy drove the buoyant Glynnis home. They walked to the doorway and he stopped, holding her hand as he spoke. "I'll call you tomorrow. Sleep well."

Glynnis touched his arm softly with her hand. "Thank you for the most wonderful day." Grace Kelly herself could not have looked more exquisite than Glynnis as she turned and went inside.

Standing inside the door, Glynnis was relieved that Susan

and Allison were nowhere in sight. She had prayed for a little time alone. Slipping noiselessly down the hallway she entered her bedroom, then leaned back against the closed door. Wild birds fluttered around her heart, scrambling furiously as if to soar away. Out of breath and feeling a little dizzy, she closed her eyes and tried to take long, relaxed breaths.

That exquisite image flooded into her head again. They stood together under the canopy of the stately tree, amidst the tropical beauty of the garden. Then Timothy leaned forward to kiss her. Glynnis flushed with pleasure and smiled. *I'll never lose that moment. For the rest of my life I will cherish it like a beautiful cameo, and each time I bring it back to my mind I will feel just like this. Over and over, forever.*

Allison sat on her bed, legs pulled up with knees pointed out, the balls of her feet touching in front, as she had done as a child. *Well, I've known I'd have to sit here by myself and come to some kind of resolution about us, but I never imagined the facts I'd be dealing with. I featured Joe momentarily distracted by some floozy, but he would eventually admit the error of his ways. What I can't figure out is how did it go from that soap opera scenario to something so mundane. I'd tried to handle the fact that he must be involved with another woman, but what I didn't expect was that a lot of doors opened up that maybe would have always remained shut if this hadn't come up. Doors that lead to problems I never realized existed. As much as I hate to say it, ours was not the perfect marriage, even before. I guess nobody has a Perfect Marriage, now that I think about it, but I would have said we did. So great, now I see my marriage isn't the fairy tale I always thought it was. And when the big crisis arrives, I can't even put on my suit of armor and go slay*

*the dragon, because there is no stupid dragon. This is so——so much a
non-crisis, so——so dull, for God's sake!*

*Of course, it could be that I'm just feeling very sorry for myself,
and that's why I've started to see some chinks in what I thought was
such a solid relationship, but I don't think so. Joe apparently sees them,
too.*

"And look at me, getting all hot under the collar like a teenager
over a handsome driver for the condo. Shades of Lady Chatterley! Is
that how I want to get my kicks? No, there's a whole lot of thinking
that I have to do to get myself straight on this one!"

*To face the very real possibility that Joe was gaga over someone else
was scary, but underneath I thought we'd work it out. We had a strong
enough love, we could and would weather a major threat. Bring in all
your courage and inner resources, pledge undying love, all that. But
this is like finding dry rot in your bathroom. It's hidden, destructive,
but pretty much just a tedious maintenance problem.*

*And what about my ego. Can I handle Joe's 'life has left me behind'
doldrums without letting the hurt affect how I feel about him? I've
compromised some pretty important stuff, and now I'm wondering why.
How come I haven't even needed to buy a new party dress in years.
That's not fair. He doesn't even care enough about me to realize I'd
have liked a little romance thrown in.*

Allison flung herself across the bed on her stomach, legs
stretched out and arms hanging down toward the floor. *Life is
a miserable joke! Joe's right, it's pretty much a letdown when you get
this far and realize that's all there is. Where's my career? Where's all the
high points, the thrills?*

She lay there sweeping the floor with a lazy hand, feeling
she'd been denied all the good things that might have been.
There was a certain comfort in this self-pity. It didn't occur to

her to cry. It wasn't a crying situation. There was no big emotion. Just a slow realization that the rainbow had faded away, or was seriously tarnished, at least. She drifted off to sleep, and only awoke an hour later when the wind blew open the window shutter, causing it to slam against the wall. Startled, it took a few minutes to come back to the present and bring the situation into focus.

But enough time had passed so that she saw things more clearly, with less emotion and self pity.

*Allison, for the love of Mike, you've really let out all your line on this one without anchoring it to anything solid. Understandable, I suppose, but enough, already. Take stock of what you have, you idiot. Whatever the present fiasco, you have a husband that you love, and who deserves to be loved. He ain't perfect, but did you ever think he was? No! Think about those children you adore—Joe does, too. And remember, lady, you and Joe are their world. There would have to be some disaster to ask them to accept a drastic change in their lives. You're talking a little monotony here. I hardly think that makes a good argument for divorce.*

*"So what if your lifestyle doesn't include a lot of parties and travel. You don't even love parties that much! Sure, that would be fun once in a while, but look at what you have. Don't tell me you don't love that place, don't enjoy tromping around in the bush with Joe and the kids. And since when did you not get a thrill out of pulling in a huge halibut or king salmon? No, it's not like dancing your heart out on a Saturday night, but don't tell me it's not a kick filling the freezer for the winter. So go ahead and feel sorry for yourself for a little while, but don't try to fool me. I know you, Allison Bradley. You're one happy lady, and don't forget it. So be honest, I don't think you have or ever will seriously consider calling it quits with Joe.*

Allison reflected on Susan and Glynnis and the patterns of their lives. Both of them undoubtedly had much more money than she. They'd grown up with it. Mom and Dad provided well for their family, but they were not in the same league, and she and Joe had done well, but there weren't many frills. What they had was immeasurable, though, and right now neither of the other women knew the bliss of a healthy, growing family and a good husband. No, whatever the shortcomings in their lives, she was lucky with her lot and whatever it took, she'd get Joe back on track.

She sighed. Finally comfortable again with her world, she lectured herself, like a coach preparing his team for a game. *It's one of those good news/bad news kinds of thing. Like going to the doctor worried you have cancer and finding out you're clear on the cancer, but that you do have a treatable ailment, and you'll need to take medication for it. I'm going to deal with the reality that life doesn't have to be full of supercharged excitement to be good. But if there are any little changes I think should be made, I'm going to have to take responsibility for making them. I'm a big girl, I can take charge where needed instead of just feeling bad that Joe didn't do it. Okay, coach. I'm raring to go. Guess I'd better tell Joe I'm back on track, and that he's going to be, too, whether he knows it or not, in spite of himself!*

She was all smiles as she dialed her husband. The phone rang several times, then Joe answered, his voice and manner so familiar, so normal.

"Hello, Joe. It's me."

"Sonny. I've been wondering how you're doing—worried about you." Joe was nervous, unsure.

"I'm fine, I've been concerned about you, too. Joe, I've

made some pretty big decisions, and discovered I need to do some things for myself."

"You can't mean it, Sonny. I was so sure you would get over all this and come back to me. I can't lose you!"

For a minute Allison lost control. "You see, Joe! That's what I mean—<u>you</u> can't lose me. Like I'm one of your customers or an airplane part. Why aren't you worried about how I'm feeling, what I'm going to do, why I've been so sad? When do I come first?" Allison sighed. "You just don't get it. You never will." But she thought a moment and then smiled, knowing this was the work that was there for her to do for herself. Before she could begin to explain her new outlook, Joe was talking, and there was new strength and determination in his voice.

"Sonny, you're at least going to hear me out. And then if you want to, you can walk away from me, our marriage, our dreams. But you'll hear what I have to say. I should have talked about it earlier, but I thought this would all blow over." He paused, realizing what Allison's reaction would be to <u>that</u> remark. "And don't say what I know you're thinking. I can call my own self a fool, you don't have to say it.

"I told you nothing happened between Rachel and me, and nothing did. No affair, I mean. But I guess something did happen in my head. I know I owe it to you to explain it all. Try to, anyway, because I don't really know what the hell was going on, either. But I'll try.

"Rachel's a really pretty girl, always most popular girl in the class all through high school. We went out a little, but there was never anything serious. Truth of the matter, she liked me a lot more than I did her. Yeah, I know what you're thinking— he's strutting again. But it's true. At any rate, when I saw her at the lab, she was still very beautiful, even after these years. And I think she still dug me. She flirted with me, kind of. Innocent, you know, but still and all, she did. And when she told me about all that was going on in her life, it sounded so much more exciting than ours. She and her husband live in a big house in Anchorage, socialize with a lot of wealthy businessmen and politicians, go to all the big bashes we read about in the newspaper, for crying out loud. It made me feel dull telling her about our life in Homer. Even though I'd always wanted just what we have, and even though she sounded pretty impressed by it. I just felt "everyday," if you know what I mean.

"So, yeah, I guess I started feeling sorry for myself, and when I got back home, I kind of found it easier to blame you for everything. And when you started suspecting that I was having an affair, that gave me a boost. Can you understand that?" Joe could hear that Allison was about to answer, and he knew it wouldn't be good. "Sonny, hold on a minute, don't say anything."

There was a loud clattering as Joe set the phone down and then shuffling noises. Music started up in the background—Willie Nelson was singing—'Maybe I didn't tell you quite as often as I should have—but you were always on my mind, you were always on my mind.'

Tears streamed uncontrolled down Allison's face. "Oh, Joe! It's okay, you see . . ."

"Sonny, I said you'd have to listen to me. I won't lose everything I love without a fight. Willie and I have become good friends since you left, and he's right, except he's singing about losing the woman he loves, and I'm not going to do that. He's right, and you're right, and all my buddies are right." He hesitated. "Yeah, I've heard about it from everybody. I've taken you for granted. It never occurred to me you might need something else but me and the kids, our home, our business, Alaska—our lives together, our dream. And there's nothing you've ever done to make my life dull. I don't know how I'd have gotten through some of the tough times if it hadn't have been for your love and your sense of humor. And you always stuck by me, no matter what. So I don't know why I ignored you so much and found it so easy to be flattered by an old girlfriend. Cabin fever, maybe. Mostly, I'm just me, no better or worse. I plead guilty.

"But remember, you're a little guilty, too, honey. Think about when I proposed to you at graduation. I told you to consider me carefully. I said I loved Alaska, probably could never leave it. I said it was hard living here—probably harder on women than men. I said to succeed in Alaska wives and husbands needed to be best friends, to trust each other—even with their lives. I said it was no-frills living, but full of beauty and happiness. I told you I wanted to carve out a flying service and that it wouldn't be glamorous, but we could make a success of all of it. And do you remember what you said?"

Allison's voice quavered. "I asked you to please quit talking, put the engagement ring on my finger and get to the kiss. Oh, Joe!"

"I'm not finished. There's more." Joe took a deep breath and plunged in. "I realize I took you for granted, it's true. That is, if taking you for granted means always depending on you being there, always knowing you loved me, that you were always the love of my life, always knowing you could make me laugh, that you'd stick out the bad times. Damn it, Sonny,

I know this isn't romantic, but you're like my lucky fishing shirt. I can crawl through thorns and branches and it'll hold up. It's warm enough to keep the wet and freezing air out, but not too hot. It doesn't take special care—I just toss it in the washing with everything else, and it comes out perfect. And yeah, it's got a few stains and snags, but to me it looks better now than it did new, and it gets more comfortable every year. And I don't even know how to explain it, but when I wear that shirt, everything is just a little better. Life is nicer.

"My dearest love, screwball that you are, you have made every moment of our time together special. I am the happiest—and luckiest—guy in all of Alaska. All of the world. Don't give up on me. Please."

Allison tried to speak, but there was a knot in her throat that didn't allow it, in fact even breathing was hard. The moment was too beautiful, too sweet, too important. And more than ever she knew she would never—no, could never—leave the man she so desperately loved. Hours could have passed, although she knew it was mere seconds.

The tiny voice that came uncertainly through the receiver warmed her heart and flooded it with old, familiar love. "Sonny, you probably deserve much better, but will you come back to me?"

"I never really left you, you ugly moose! But you just compared me to a shirt that should have been donated to the ragbag years ago. For that you owe me a night on the town!" Her voice became solemn, subdued. "I'm coming home, Joe. I guess I always knew I would. How could I be anywhere else?"

*Chapter Ten*

# Thursday Evening

**It was evening** when the three got together in the living room. As Allison described the results of her conversation, a mood of celebration filled the room.

The honesty that was Allison's trademark shone through, "I know we were never really off track. But we took a broadside hit and discovered that nobody lives a charmed life or has a perfect marriage, not even us. And it was sobering to find out just how easy it is to slip into some bad thinking. Joe did it, and then I did it, too. When you allow the clouds to come into your life and cover the sunshine, you forget all the good and focus on the little disappointments, until some of them loom pretty large and scary on your horizon. It takes work to keep that from happening, but it's worth every bit of effort.

"I don't want to sound too much like a Pollyanna, but as tough as this time has been, it's helped me understand something about myself, and it will help me in the future. Part of the reason I've wanted a little more pizzazz in our marriage is that I do feel cheated that I dropped all my career dreams. I'd do it again, you'd better believe it, but underneath I still yearn to do something with my training and whatever ability may still be in this tired head. Until now it wasn't practical to think about it, but perhaps I can look at some options. Maybe there are some writing opportunities right at home, and I would need to take some refresher courses to get back into sync.

Bottom line, though, I'll have to look at how it affects our family and finances. Instead of feeling bent out of shape because Joe hasn't supported me on this, it's time I grew up and took the responsibility on myself to see if I can work it out. Honestly, I know if I can show him that it would work, he'd back me. So tune in a year or so from now to see if I've had the willpower to do anything.

"And wrestling with the need for more wallop to life, Joe just went through it, but I've pined away for more glamour and excitement for years. I just didn't let it show. Well, we can't have it all, and I guess I have pretty close to everything. I'll just have to pass on the daily dose of romance. Joe's never going to place a rose by my morning coffee or drop a little diamond trinket in my glass of champagne to surprise me. For us lucky ones, that's the bad news. I'm sure Joe wishes he didn't have to worry over the books each month to make sure we're solvent. He'd most likely choose to lay back and relax if he could. I lost sight of how fortunate I am if that's the biggest worry. We all face certain compromises, and ours are small ones."

"I'd say you're both older and wiser. And we're bursting with happiness for you—if not a little jealous!" Susan smiled. "But as an attorney, I should warn you that the downside of this resolution of your marital problem is that it's probably going to shorten your time here. I'm not sure we want to allow your future happiness and fulfillment to so seriously jeopardize our fledgling coalition!"

"Well, all the more reason to get going with our vacation plans. We'll just pack more into every day." Allison's solution made everyone smile.

"As if we could! We need a full-time Activities Director

as it is, don't you agree, Glynnis?" Susan could sense her days were going to be fuller than the other two imagined.

Allison didn't miss a beat. "So let's stop dawdling and wasting precious time. We should be planning!"

"Well, for starters, you might both like a day at Ala Moana, that large mall in Honolulu. That is, if you want to do any gift shopping for people at home. There are dozens of wonderful shops there, you name it, it's there. And being surrounded by the crowds is fabulous. I could spend hours there watching the rest of the world walk by." Susan thought briefly and continued.

"Or we could drive around the Island, go up to the North Shore into the country and where all the surfing is done, look at some of laid-back towns unlike any you've seen so far, and circle right back to downtown Honolulu. You'd get a better idea of the whole island.

"If you'd prefer, there are a lot of events organized for tourists. We might go hang-gliding, learn how to hula, sign up for a luau!" The ideas made Allison laugh, but Glynnis was more serious.

"I think Alesa might organize a luau for us, so I'd rather not do that, Susan. Especially since, if Alesa is in charge, we could be a little surer of what we'd be eating. I've read about some typical luau dishes that are a little . . . unusual."

"Well, then we're down to two choices, a trip around the Island, or mall shopping. Unless there's something else that has caught your interest." Susan looked at Glynnis and Allison for their reaction.

"I know I can't go home without shopping. Sound okay? Then maybe we'll still have time the next day for the North Shore. I don't know yet when I can get a reservation."

A jangling telephone interrupted Allison's suggestion, and suspended the decision-making process. Timothy was calling for Glynnis. She took the telephone and walked around the corner into the semi-privacy of the kitchen as the others smiled.

"I just wanted to say hello, and ask if you could spend some time with me tomorrow. I wish we could take the entire day, but believe it or not, I am a working man. But could I pick you up around three o'clock? I thought you might like to see the zoo, if you haven't been there already."

"What a wonderful idea! I hope it will work." Glynnis hesitated. "You see, Allison is leaving soon, so we want to do as much as possible together while she's here. We were just talking about going to Ala Moana shopping center to buy gifts for friends. Susan recommends it. I would love to see the zoo with you, really I would, but I don't know . . ."

"Don't turn me down! I have a plan. Suppose I pick you up at 3 o'clock at Ala Moana, and from there it's only a short way to the zoo. We'll spend a couple of hours there, and I'll put you right back down at the shopping center to be with your friends again. How about that?" Tim's voice was eager.

"Well . . ."

"It'll work. Trust me. And may I take you and your friends to the spot I mentioned for dinner and music? I talked to Alesa and she can make it. How about you?"

"You go so fast, I can't seem to argue with you! Wait just a minute, while I check with Allison and Susan." Within minutes she was back, laughing. "They say yes, they can hardly wait." She hesitated. "I think they are curious about you. Isn't that silly!"

"Not at all. Friends watch out for friends. And I promise you, I will be such a gentleman, they won't be able to disapprove of me. I'll pull out all the stops."

"Now you are being silly. After all, we're just newly acquainted friends, that's all. I'm more than a little concerned that they think I'm acting a bit impetuous. After all, I've just met you, and already I've gone off alone with you—it's all been quite mysterious, I might add. I'm not really sure I understand my behavior, let alone explain it to them." Glynnis fussed nervously at her hair.

"No one who's known you for even one hour could possibly believe you'd do anything that wasn't completely honorable, Glynnis. And don't forget, these are special circumstances. We may have just met, but we've had a connection all our lives. Doesn't that change the situation a little bit?"

A smile crept over her face. "I suppose you're right. And of course, I want my friends to meet Alesa." Her smile faded, and she bit her lip. "I hope you don't become bored with me because I'm cautious and indecisive. You couldn't really call me spontaneous. Tedious would be an accurate description, perhaps."

"Hey, sorry to have to disagree, but I consider you charming and fun to be around. With a touch of intrigue and mystery thrown in. Where do you get the notion you'd be boring?"

The worry lines still etched her forehead, despite Tim's words of approval. As she spoke, her voice lacked energy. "If you had known me longer, you would understand that I've always been afraid and cautious, and I've never just taken up with a near-stranger before. Since coming on this trip to Hawaii, so much has changed for me—meeting my new friends the moment we arrived at the airport. They have done so much to show me how to enjoy life more. Then learning about Alesa. I am very fortunate for these changes to my life, but I'm not sure I know how to handle it all. And even though I feel happier than ever before, I worry that it's just an illusion. Perhaps everyone feels this happy and renewed on vacation, and then when it's over, everything reverts back to the way it was. I really don't want that to happen, but I am a little afraid that's what's ahead. How could it change?" Glynnis paused, embarrassed. "I'm sorry for boring you with all this. It's certainly not your concern."

"There's that word 'boring' again. Sooner or later I'm going to find the way to convince you that you're wrong. That's just going to require that we see more of each other! So we'll start today, right?" Timothy set up a meeting place for the next day and they said their good-byes.

## Chapter Eleven

# Friday

**"It's Aloha Friday,** everyone!" Susan smiled when Glynnis and Allison came down the hallway and hugged them as she presented each with a lei. "Noelani made these up this morning. Aren't they wonderful?" As they admired the compact trumpet-shaped flowers of light gold, Susan added, "They're called Pua Kenikeni. It means 10¢ flowers. In the old days, they became favorite lei flowers because of their marvelous fragrance, but also because they were so inexpensive . . . ten cents apiece."

"Oh, they're lovely! And I know a little about Aloha Friday. Timothy explained to me that people here give leis to one another every Friday simply to show their friendship. Hawaiian people are so caring, aren't they?"

"Huh! You're getting quite an education in Hawaiian history and customs, Glyn. Lucky you, you found yourself a fella!"

"Allison! I haven't 'found myself a fella.' You know he's just a friend. And remember, he is inviting you and the rest of us to dinner tonight, so practice being on your best behavior! You mustn't think you can embarrass me and get away with it, even if you are about to leave. Susan will help me find a way to retaliate, won't you, Susan?" Glynnis' stern admonition was accompanied by a wide smile.

"Why naturally I will! We can't have Allison having all the fun around here. Maybe we'll hide your ticket, so you're marooned on this island. And we'll tell your husband you've decided to run away with a wealthy plantation owner. That should put you in plenty of hot water!" Susan's teasing made everyone laugh.

"All right, all right. I'll be on my best behavior, but I think we should at least be able to grill this guy. Find out what his intentions are and all that. That's okay, isn't it?"

"Allison, you're impossible! But I don't believe your threats, not for a minute. So have your fun, I'm onto you."

They quickly put together what was needed for the day. Susan took the condo car after checking with Eric that it was available. First, though, they took a drive along the coast.

"Doesn't seem to matter which way we go, it's like a travelogue everywhere. I love this coastline. It's so different from Alaska. Not just the scenery. Of course they're both indescribably beautiful, but there's worlds of difference. Homer is on Kachemak Bay, protected. We don't have the exciting surf like this. Of course, we get some pretty amazing tides. Would you believe 20 feet? But it doesn't look or feel like this, even if you eliminate the tropical plants on the coastline. And I'm used to sea ducks and Alaskan birds, lots of gulls and terns, murres and puffins. One of my favorite places in the bay is Bird Island, where the puffins and murres nest and breed. There aren't too many shore birds here. I can understand why. Who would want to fly the thousands of miles out to sea to get here! But what I've seen—the stormy petrel, the frigatebird—I've gotten pretty fond of them. Joe would get a kick out of watching them.

"Would you care to compare the temperature of the water in both places, Allison?" Susan laughed. "In fact, we should do some scientific research on that subject. Maybe tomorrow? We could drive over to Hanauma Bay. You can't leave the Islands without going there. Of course, every tourist that flies in visits the bay, but who can blame them. It's a preserve, protected, so the fish are there by the thousands. We'll take snorkel masks and you'll be able to see tropical fish eye to eye. It's unforgettable. Use plenty of sunscreen, though. The sun is intense. I can't wait to introduce you to this place. You're going to have the experience of a lifetime."

"I've been admiring pictures of tropical fish in the travel literature. It's hard to believe we'll actually see them." Glynnis became tentative. "Do you think it's safe to go out in the water? Are there sharks?"

"Glynnis, I won't say there have never been sharks in that bay or anywhere else on the Island, but they don't usually come in, because it's inside the reefs. It's like flying in an airplane. Certainly accidents happen, but the chances are almost nil. And when you think of the thousands of people who go in that water every week, you know the odds are stacked against anything happening to you."

"We can live a little, can't we, Glynn? Take our chances with the next guy? Look danger square in the eye!" Allison noticed her joking wasn't going over that well. "Sorry, my friend. I was just making light of it to be funny. Listen, I wouldn't put my toe in that water if I thought there was any chance of something biting it off. I believe Susan. She wouldn't lead us astray. And we've looked down on that bay from the road and seen so many people there you couldn't even see the beach. It's gotta be safe. Let's do it!" Glynnis drew a deep breath and nodded her hesitant agreement.

"All right. So we're going to Hanauma Bay tomorrow. You won't regret it, I guarantee. And I know where we can rent an underwater camera to take some of our own nature photos, Glynnis!" They agreed it would be a day to remember, and Susan drove on to the mall.

Their shopping trip turned into almost a party, each one discovering new shops and delighting in finding unusual gifts. Allison had no trouble finding things for her children, a samurai sword and outfit for Bobby and a hula skirt with plastic flower leis for Jill. She bought them books about Hawaiian birds, fish, and flowers, as well as short histories and a wonderful book of legends, wanting them to learn about Hawaii. Of course there had to be T-shirts for everyone, and she laughed as she picked one out for Joe that proclaimed "Surf's Up!" "He'll hate it, but maybe I can talk him into wearing it. And I know he'll love the old engraved knife I found for him. "Hmm, I wonder if I should buy HIM a hula skirt. After watching that program on TV last night featuring male hula dancers, I think he'd look pretty good! Well, now that I think about it, unless he came here to get a tan first, I'm afraid not. Too much white skin." She found a nut dish made of local koa wood for her parents that she knew would please them. "And for me, I'm going home with some CDs of that wonderful Hawaiian music, so I won't be so lonesome for this place. Or maybe it will make me even more lonesome, but I want them, anyway."

Glynnis found a couple of old Hawaiian prints to send to Uncle John, knowing that nothing she did for him could adequately acknowledge what he had accomplished by demanding she come on this trip. "What a good man. I'll never be able to thank him enough."

Alesa's gift presented the challenge. Glynnis worried about what it should be, wanting it to be perfect. But knowing and loving the woman's home as she did, she decided to browse through all the stores until something caught her eye. She would know the right thing when she saw it. It surprised her that instead of feeling any pressure, she truly enjoyed looking for something that would fit into the wonderful home. She fell in love with a delicate Japanese teapot of unusual shape and design with striking colors. What intrigued her most was the use of intertwined gnarled willow boughs for the handle in contrast to the classic porcelain pot. Proud of her discovery, she enjoyed the rest of the time watching Allison complete her shopping. Susan bought nothing, and told them very casually that she had long ago bought everything Hawaiian that she could possibly use. But she looked discreetly at baby things and mementos of this important time, and made a resolution to come back later to buy.

"Why, where has the time gone? I'm supposed to meet Timothy in just a few minutes." Glynnis described their prearranged meeting spot and Susan guided them there. Timothy spied them and came over from his parked car. After being introduced to Allison and discussing plans for the dinner party, he guided Glynnis to his car and they pulled away, leaving Allison and Susan smiling.

"Nice fellow, isn't he?" Susan nodded approvingly as she watched them leave.

"Boy, I've got to hand it to Glynnis. She can really pick 'em. And we thought she was so shy. Methinks we're not the only ones who have seen what a neat lady she is. He can't be too bad a guy if he appreciates what he's got."

"We're beginning to sound like matchmakers. My mother told me once that matchmaking is not unlike making a wish. You may think you are wishing for something quite beautiful, but never forget, with a wish you never have control over the outcome, and you can't be quite sure how it will be accomplished. Maybe we'd better let this relationship mature on its own!"

"You think I want to meddle? Me? You know I do! But you're probably right. We'd better not mess with something that looks like it's shaping up without any interference from us! It's tempting, though. Especially when I'm going to be going so soon. And with Glynnis planning to leave right after, it could just evaporate right before our eyes." Allison looked at Susan to see any sign of approval for their nudging the couple a little.

"Let me paraphrase what I know my mother would warn: 'One sometimes feels that one has the obligation to manage situations. One must, however, remember that if one does butt in, one must further agree to be there to pick up the pieces if all goes astray.' But I have to admit, I couldn't bear for all this to end with a poignant farewell at the airport, with Glynnis going back to a fairly colorless future in Philadelphia and this opportunity becoming just a memory. I guess we should pay careful attention to what goes on at dinner tonight. We need all the information we can gather. Still staying out of it, of course, you understand."

"Gotcha. We'll do whatever it takes to make this thing happen before it's too late. Right?"

"Your words, not mine. Now let's go get something to eat. I'm starved."

Timothy was all smiles as Glynnis slid into his car. He produced a striking lei of plumeria blossoms.

"Oh, heavens, I already have this lei that Susan gave me this morning."

"The mark of someone who's loved—or liked a lot. You can wear two, sweet thing. It's not a crime, in fact, the more the merrier, until you have a hard time breathing when they cover your face. Besides, you're making my day, a beautiful lady wearing my favorite flowers. I can't ask for more." Timothy paused. "Really."

The couple drove through Waikiki and along the beach until they reached the zoo. For two hours they delighted in watching the animals, and even more especially, the children and families who were also enjoying a day out. Glynnis laughed as Tim showed her around, commenting on all there was to see. They stopped for a soft drink and hot dog on the lawn under the shady canopy of a huge poinciana tree and asked a passerby to take their picture with Timothy's camera.

"Now we'll be part of Alesa's scrapbook, too." Glynnis blushed and smiled as she pictured their photo in the pages of family history.

"Well, this will be the first. We've got to make sure there are more, lots more. Alesa loves pictures, as you've seen!" Timothy hesitated, then continued. "Alesa told me she would like you to stay here on the island a while longer with her. She doesn't want to see you go so soon. I don't either. She is reluctant to ask you—wouldn't want to interfere or anything. But I don't want her shyness to prevent you from knowing how she feels. I admit to being a little selfish about this. You've come here and taken over a little place in our hearts. I want to convince you to stay."

Glynnis' heart jumped, but she took a deep breath and

continued with honesty. "Oh, that is so considerate of both of you. Alesa is very generous. But my plans are already made. I must get back to—well, to business and my home. There's a lot to catch up with. I never planned to be here more than just a short time."

"You couldn't have known what was going to happen when you got here. I don't know for sure how you feel, but I definitely don't want you to go flying off on an airplane. But look, don't think about it right now. Don't try to decide. Let the idea take hold a little, and you can talk more to Alesa tonight." He laughed, "You've traveled all this way, you've met an exciting, handsome man. Why cut it short and leave me in the dust, unless you really want to hurt me!" Seeing Glynnis smile, he continued more seriously, "We should take the time to know one another better. I think it's important. But as I told you, don't feel you have to decide just yet."

"Oh, dear. Complications. Life was never this complex before. Well, I won't decide now. I promise I'll think about it, at least consider it a little. I suppose nothing is carved in stone, even plane reservations."

"That's good enough for me right now. You just keep thinking that way. Now, I'd better get you back to your friends. I want you to have plenty of time to get ready for tonight."

Glynnis was cheerful as she, Susan and Allison traveled back home to prepare for the evening. She felt a buoyancy, a new excitement about her life. If only this could be something more than a temporary mood. What if she was steering her life in a refreshing new direction! She remembered an actress from many classic movies, what was her name? Always perfectly poised, wise, and always a dignified demeanor no matter what problems might assail her. Greer Garson, that was it! So distinguished and gracious as she and the schoolmaster fell in love in "Goodbye, Mr. Chips," noble and quietly proud in the war story, "Mrs. Miniver." Could she be so happy, even giddy, inside and still retain that Greer Garson image to the rest of the world? Time would tell!

Everyone was excited about dinner. It was going to be a wonderful night, and they anticipated a good time.

Lanterns shed soft light on the garden area around the golf club restaurant, enhancing the beauty of the landscaping. The three women met Timothy and Alesa and after introductions were made, they went in and were seated at a table near the piano. Susan instantly recognized it. She and her parents had come there many years before. "What a good choice." Susan smiled. "Do you come here often, Alesa?"

"Oh, no. I don't really go out to restaurants too often anymore. Family and my home take up most of my time, but I know I will enjoy this evening." Alesa's eyes twinkled with delight.

As they looked at the menu and discussed what they would order, Glynnis was fascinated by the roomful of people. Very unlike the restaurants they'd been to so far, this one presented a comfortable, homey atmosphere. It was apparent the guests were not tourists, which made her a trifle nervous. She didn't like to intrude on their domain. But it was nice to be in a family setting.

A young man sitting directly across the room caught her attention. He was heavy-set, probably in his early twenties. Glynnis thought he was more than likely Hawaiian, or perhaps

Polynesian. What troubled her was his brooding appearance. She sensed his defiance. He didn't smile much, didn't join in the conversation at his table. Still not totally comfortable in unfamiliar situations, Glynnis was disquieted by his presence, sure he was staring at her. This was a boy who might have a violent nature, and who could tell what he had on his mind. She thought back to another man and his failed bomb attempt in Waikiki the day of her arrival.

She spoke quietly. "That young man across the room worries me. He seems so sullen and dark, as though he has a chip on his shoulder and is just waiting for someone to try to challenge him. Do you think he's dangerous?"

Timothy's eyes flickered just a little with a smile, but he responded to Glynnis' worried comments sincerely. "Often Hawaiians are more shy than you'd expect. You may be confusing a little embarrassment for an attitude. I don't believe you have to worry, especially since you have a personal bodyguard with you tonight!"

That relieved the tension. Anyway, she couldn't stay worried very long, because there was happy conversation around her table, and a feeling of high gaiety. Stories were told, secrets shared. Alesa embarrassed Timothy by telling the story of the time when, at age five, thinking of himself as the great Hawaiian King Kamehameha, he fashioned a canoe out of a cardboard carton to carry him to the other islands. He set out from the beach, but his fine "boat" soon became soggy and the family watched as it slowly filled with water and sank just a few feet from shore.

"It didn't seem very funny at the time, but I guess it made me want to learn to swim right away! And now that I think about the scene, it must have looked pretty funny." Tim smiled. "What the heck, I'll do anything to make people smile."

Dinner proceeded with more laughter and exclamations of how fine the meal was. A handsome man strolled out to the piano and began the evening's entertainment, playing and singing song after wonderful song. He had a seemingly unlimited repertoire, and his music delighted everyone. Soon he began calling people up from the audience, and each contributed to the musical night. Some sang, others strummed a ukulele, a grandfather played ukulele and sang while his small granddaughter danced hula. After many had come up to perform, the piano player stopped and spoke into his microphone. "We haven't heard from my friend Keolu yet tonight. Come up and sing something for us." Eyes moved around the room to see where Keolu might be.

To Glynnis' shock and consternation, it appeared that Keolu was the angry young man who was the cause of her unease. He stood up, and she realized he was even taller and bigger than she had imagined. Without smiling he lumbered directly past her, brushing her shoulder as he went by, steadfastly staring at the floor, until he stood in the center of the small stage, next to the piano. With serious face and no introduction, he said quietly, "I'd like to sing my favorite song. It's one my tutu sang to me." And his was the sweetest voice, simple and true. When he finished, many of the older ladies wiped their eyes, touched by his rendition.

"Holy mackerel. I never heard anything so beautiful. He should be a recording artist!" Allison looked toward Glynnis. "Your gangster may be on the Most Wanted list, but he sure has one terrific voice."

"I'm overwhelmed. That was amazing. And if I remember,

tutu means grandmother. He sang the song his grandmother sang to him. So touching, and I thought he was going to mug us or something worse. I guess I'm still learning about a whole different way of life."

"That's why, Glynnis dear, you need to stay here awhile with me, learn a little more about us. There's so much we could share together. Timmy told me he explained my hope that you'd stay, and he made me promise I wouldn't pressure you. And I won't. But please know that from the bottom of my heart, it would make me so happy if you'd consider staying awhile. And don't think I won't put you to work. I've got projects already lined up for both of us to do!" There was hope in Alesa's voice.

"I promise to consider it, Alesa. Seriously consider it. I'll tell you very soon." Glynnis' eyes moved from Alesa to Timothy, her message meant for both.

They finished their dessert and coffee and, tired but content, they left, still laughing and commenting on what a perfect evening it had been.

Allison walked up to Timothy as they approached the cars. "I'm afraid we're going to commandeer Glynnis tomorrow. I have reservations to fly home the next day, so tomorrow we're going to Hanauma Bay. A kind of farewell party. But I do want to tell you how much we think of that girl, how much we've grown attached in such a little time. I really care what happens to her, and so does Susan. Whether she stays here or not is Glynnis' decision, but personally, I hope she takes Alesa up on her offer. I think she's very happy here. You take care that she stays happy, hear?" So saying, Allison patted Tim on the arm and went cheerfully to her car.

*Chapter Twelve*

# Saturday

**"This is the** most perfect day I have ever seen!" Allison had been outside on the patio long before the other two were up. "I know that every day is 'just another ho-hum perfect day in Paradise' here, but this one's impossibly great. Look at the color on the mountains, and that breeze is heavenly. I may have to tell Joe and the kids to come get me. No way can a sane person think of leaving this."

"Well, you deserve the best. It's our way of showing you how much we care about you." Glynnis looked at Susan. "We couldn't let Allison go without a glorious sendoff, isn't that right?"

"I must admit, this is some beautiful day. And we'll squeeze every bit of fun out of it that we can. No stopping until late tonight, promise?" Susan felt particularly lighthearted since she had talked to her parents before going to bed the night before, and now planned to break her good news about Philip and keeping the baby to Allison and Glynnis when they got to the beach. She knew she must be absolutely glowing, even without makeup, this morning. "And so, without wasting another minute, let's get ready to go. Noelani has packed a hamper with food for a brunch at the beach, and as a special treat, and because you can't leave without experiencing them, we're picking up one of Hawaii's best and most sinful treats, malasadas from Leonard's Bakery in Honolulu. I've told them we'll pick them up in an hour, and that way they'll be freshly made just as we get there."

"And what might malasadas be, may I ask?"You've got my curiosity up, and I can see that Glynnis wants to make sure that whatever they are, they're not raw and they don't come from deep under the sea!" Allison laughed.

"Oh, you have nothing to worry about. Malasadas are wonderful, fattening Portuguese fried doughnuts. They are not on anybody's list of diet foods, but once in awhile, you've got to break the rules, right?

"You're right, Susan. I think we three have been very careful up to now, when you consider how many tempting foods we've seen. We can afford to splurge." No one disagreed with Glynnis' justification, even though they silently acknowledged many glorious diversions from the path of healthful eating.

It didn't take long for them to be organized and on their way. The stop near Waikiki at the bakery proved what Susan said. The malasada order was ready within minutes of their arrival. With the car full of the enticing aroma escaping from the bakery box, they hurried on to the bay, loaded their arms with their hamper and towels and trudged toward the path that led to the beach. Before starting down the trail from the parking lot, Glynnis and Allison stopped, astonished at what lay below. A near-perfect circle of cove, an extinct volcano crater, adorned with a swatch of white beach, cradled its startling treasure of luminous turquoise water. Outside the bay, the water became rough and currents rushed under the sea, reason enough for scores of tropical fish to be drawn here to its quiet protection.

There was only a handful of people on the beach, since the

three had come early to get ahead of the crowds. The water was like crystal, tattooed with a dark maze of coral reefs below.

The excited trio proceeded down the rocky stairs toward the beach, with Susan leading them toward a comfortable spot to picnic. Towels were spread out and Susan brought out a thermos of coffee, cups, plates and the tantalizing malasadas. They laughed and ate, groaning with pleasure.

"All I can say, Sue, is that we wouldn't have had a clue what to do, where to go or what to eat if you hadn't adopted us this last week. I know all the tourists we've seen are having a wonderful time, but I don't think their trip has been anything like ours. This was the Blue Ribbon Treatment, for sure." Allison looked at Susan. "And we haven't forgotten that you've had some things on your mind all this while. We would have understood if you'd driven us to some road, dumped us out of the car, and gone home alone for some solitude."

"Allison's right, Susan." Glynnis looked at their hostess with a look of seriousness. "You have given up all your time to see that we enjoyed our trip. You haven't done a thing for yourself. We are so lucky you took us in, but you should have thought more about your own needs."

Susan smiled broadly. "I wouldn't say I haven't done anything for myself, ladies. We have kept pretty busy, I'll grant you, but during breaks in our activities I have made some pretty important and dramatic changes. Everything that was confused and jarring in my life has resolved itself. Philip and I are going to be married—right here—in a few days, and then we are going to wait for the birth of our baby. The two of us. Just like it was meant to be." Tears sprang to her eyes, tears of delight.

"Oh, Susan, you don't know how relieved I am. I have suffered so thinking about your dilemma. I knew you would be wise and find a good solution, but in all my dreams I didn't know you could resolve it so beautifully. I could weep with happiness." Glynnis' eyes became wide. "Then it looks like I really will be an auntie . . . sort of."

"You two will be Aunties of the first order. And that means we'll expect regular visits so you can check how your niece or nephew is doing, considering that the poor baby is being entrusted to someone who may be more clown than good mother. Thank goodness Phil is used to children and knows what to do. He'll keep everything held together when you're not around!"

Allison was strangely subdued, but her face shone with happiness. "I don't know quite what to say. Ever since you told us about what was going on, I've tried to put myself in your position. I ached so much for you, hoping you would keep the baby. But it wasn't my place to say anything, and not only that, who can decide what's best for someone else? In reality, we hardly know each other, but over this week we have all become so close. It's strange, perhaps we were all at a place in our lives where it was more helpful to be away from our close friends and family and work through our problems with people who didn't have preconceived ideas about us.

"In my case, everyone always thinks I'm on top of everything, just because I seem to be able to stay cool in most situations. But that doesn't mean I've got all the answers or that I always know how to deal with life. I think my friends would have expected me to be in control way more than I was. You two just accepted me and my story and showed me your support without assuming anything.

"Glynnis, you've changed right before our eyes. But don't get me wrong, there's nothing new about you, it's always been part of you. You've merely allowed a little more to come out. You're more comfortable with who you are, and who you are is somebody great.

"And Mother Susan, you have been quietly in the background with your anguish. Oh, you let us know about it, and I'm glad you did. But you obviously didn't want a lot of input from us. You are an independent lady, and I know it took a lot for you to open up as you did. I hope it helped a little to do that. It looks to me like you were battling more than just the knowledge that you were pregnant. I think a lot of battles were being waged in your mind while we were laughing and playing. I prayed you would decide to keep the baby. I never had a clue that in the end you would bring this whole thing together—husband, baby, family, forever and evermore. Hats off to you!" Allison cried as she gave Susan a hug, then lightened her mood. "Maybe you should give up lawyering and become a screenwriter! And I don't know Philip, but you tell him he's a lucky man! And darn it, I won't be here to give him my top sergeant inspection like I did Tim."

"Okay, I think we've had enough emotion to last us the rest of the morning! Let's get the snorkels and I'll introduce you to some beautiful tropical fish. And don't forget the underwater camera!" Susan led them to the water's edge. She gave a brief lesson on how to use the snorkels and how to maneuver over the coral in shallow water. "It's sometimes just a matter of hand-over-hand moving yourself along, because you're only in a little water. Just don't go out too far. When you get out near the opening of the bay things change and beyond that it's very rough. The current out there is nicknamed the Molokai Express because it rushes directly toward the island of Molokai. You don't want to take that ride! And you don't need to go very far at all to see every fish you could ever imagine—Moorish Idols, tangs, surgeonfish, wrasses, wonderful pipefish. Pufferfish that you'll love. If you don't know exactly what it is you're looking at, I brought an identification book. We'll look them up later."

For an hour the three were lost in the underwater playground. Occasionally one would signal to the others, gesturing about something they had seen. The others would wave and return to their search. Finally Susan, feeling very tired suddenly, waved to the others, signaling to meet on the beach.

Once they were lying on their beach towels they broke into excited conversation, especially Glynnis and Allison, who wanted to describe each fish they'd seen. They compared their discoveries animatedly, hardly believing what had appeared right before their eyes.

As they talked, Susan brought out snacks from the hamper, and they relaxed awhile, catching their breath and resting. They applied more sunblock and stretched out to enjoy the warm sun.

Half an hour passed before Susan nudged the others. "You may think we're finished, but we've got more to do. I want to show you some special places around the bay that a lot of people don't know about. Like the Toilet Bowl, for instance."

"This I've gotta see! Or maybe I don't even want to know about it." Allison was skeptical, wondering if Susan was pulling their leg.

"It sounds a little disgusting, if you ask me." Glynnis couldn't imagine there was such a place.

"I'm not fooling you. It's up around the cliffs over there. It's a hole in the lava with a tidepool inside. Also there's an inlet at the bottom where waves surge in and that fills the hole. Then when the wave pulls back, it empties. Toilet bowl effect. Be careful, though, when we're walking around there. Sometimes the waves pound in very powerfully and splash over the trail, and you can slip if you're not careful. People do get hurt out here, so be careful, okay?"

It was quite a hike to the hole. Allison and Glynnis enjoyed this new view of the bay and surroundings, and stopped at each turn to admire the beauty. Susan was tired and felt faint. *Too much physical activity, I guess. As soon as we do this, I'll drive us home and take a nap.*

"So here we are. Watch a minute and you can see what I was telling you . . ." Her sentence was interrupted by the roar of a wave forcing its way into the small bowl. They roared with delight as the bowl filled with foaming water, then flushed back down as the wave receded.

"It's such a joy to think of bringing our baby here in the years to come. Enjoying this kind of day with Phil and our little one." Susan laughed as she spun around to hold out her arms as though to capture the whole bay in her thoughts.

The wave that jammed into the rocks and through the lava into the bowl was huge, catching them off guard. Glynnis stumbled, then righted herself as hard spray hit them. Allison braced her feet to keep upright, although she was drenched.

Susan staggered forward, unbalanced and dizzy at the same time. She seemed to be floating in mid-air instead of falling, her joyful smile frozen on her face. There was intense ringing in her ears, then it was strangely quiet. The world had left her behind somewhere, and gone on without her.

Allison and Glynnis looked on in horror as Susan tumbled into the bowl as it churned and then ebbed noisily out to sea. She appeared lifeless, rolled and thrust into the rocks at the will of the wave. It was a cruel cage of sharp lava, jagged and unyielding and the unconscious body had no weapon to fight back when the next wave assaulted her. Terrified, they scrambled down into the pit and quickly, not knowing what to do or how they would accomplish anything, they half pushed, half pulled her out of the perilous cauldron, back up onto the pathway. Fearing another wave too large to be contained in the bowl, they dragged Susan back to a safe spot.

"Stay with her, Glynnis. I'm going for help." Allison didn't wait for a reply, she set off running.

Glynnis covered her friend with the towel she had worn sarong-style on the walk. Susan lay still and white, but she was breathing. There were terrible cuts and scratches all over her body, and blood was flowing from several gashes. Glynnis could only dab at them with the corner of the towel. It didn't seem to do much good. Tears were falling down her cheeks and her body shook with fear. This couldn't be happening. But she must remain calm and take care of Susan. Lying down close to her she tried to shield her stricken friend and keep her warm. She cradled her and crooned softly, reassuring her it would be all right. She was there and would stay there with her. Help would come. Allison would bring someone.

Glynnis didn't stop her soothing talk until Allison came running back.

"They're going to land a helicopter right on that shoulder over there. It's the quickest way. And they'll transport her to the hospital."

The paramedics arrived with the 'copter and soon they were flying over the unforgettable Hanauma Bay on a grotesque trip, possibly a life and death mission.

Glynnis was jolted by a thought and spoke quickly to the paramedics. "You should know, Miss Michaels is pregnant. It's imperative you work to save both her and her baby." The medics looked bleakly back. Glynnis and Allison exchanged glances of disbelief.

At last they landed on the hospital roof and began what was more nightmare than reality.

## Chapter Thirteen

# Later Saturday

**The hospital corridor** was filled with doctors and nurses flowing one way and the other, a stage set for drama. Susan lay very still in her room, and just outside her friends sat, leaden and weary. Someone had thoughtfully found hospital bathrobes for them when they noticed the two huddled in bathing suits and shaking with shock and anxiety. An orderly brought them coffee, which sat untouched on the table between them.

Allison straightened. "I need to do some phoning. Susan's parents should know, and Philip. I can't tell them how she is doing, because nobody has said a bloody thing. But they have to know. I'll come right back, Glynny. Don't let the doctor go by without talking to him. They must know something by now."

"Yes." Glynnis' eyes were focused on the door of Susan's room. She didn't look at Allison, simply acknowledged that she had heard.

And when Allison returned after a half-hour, Glynnis looked up briefly, shrugged her shoulders, and shifted her eyes back to the closed door. "The doctor stopped to talk for just a moment. He didn't tell me much, just that Susan is still unconscious and has lost a lot of blood. He wouldn't tell me anything about the baby. Only that it was a critical time right now. And that he must go back. And he left. Did you make the phone calls?"

"I realized I had no idea how to call anybody, so I called Eric. He's in shock, as you'd expect. He looked up Philip's number, but Susan's notebook showed that her parents left this morning for St. Louis. They're in the air right now. So I called Philip." Allison stared at the tile floor. "That was the hardest conversation I've ever had. I don't have to tell you how he feels. He's catching the first plane he can get and will be here as soon as possible.

"I called Joe and my folks and told them I couldn't come home tomorrow. They understand, of course. And I called Timothy and told him. I hope you don't mind. But I figured it would help. He's not too far away. He'll close things up and be here as soon as he can."

A nurse came over to them. "I know you're worried so about your friend. I wish I could tell you something, but you just have to keep praying and wait. Everything possible is being done, and she's in good hands. It's so hard to just sit here with nothing to do. Let me show you a little room right over there," she signaled to an alcove just down the corridor. "You'd be more comfortable there, I think. It's private and there are comfortable armchairs and a couple of sofas in case you care to lie down. There's even a television. It would make the time go faster to have a little distraction."

"But we need to be here, close to her room, in case there are any changes." Glynnis was adamant.

"You can keep your eye on the door from there. And I promise you, I will let everyone know where you are and if there is anything to tell you, we'll find you." And like a worried mother, the nurse led them by the hand to the quiet room and got them situated.

"I guess we're here for a long time, yeah? I've got to tell you, I'm not fond of hospitals." Allison looked tense.

"I spent a lot of time in them when Mother was ill and then with Father. I don't like them, either, but when they suddenly become part of your daily routine, they become bearable. You find yourself setting up a schedule to work with events and decisions you couldn't have imagined just days before." Memories from short months before clouded Glynnis' mind.

"Oh, Glyn, I forgot you'd just gone through so much with your parents. This must be harder than ever for you."

"How could anything make this harder than it is? What's happening is unspeakably wrong. But we both have to be here, living through it, wishing it weren't so. We haven't any choice. The only thing we have control over is that we can devote every scrap of energy we have to helping Susan."

Quietly, Allison looked at Glynnis with understanding and admiration. "I know."

The nurse looked in on them. "I see you haven't budged since you came in here. You need a little break. Why don't you walk down to the cafeteria and get a bite of something? I promise I'll come get you if there's any news." When she saw they were ready to object, she continued. "Your friend is lucky to have you two here. But look here, you're not going to be worth very much to her if you're out on your feet. You need to take care of yourselves, for her sake. Do you know it's been over four hours since you came in? Go. I'll let you know."

They heard wisdom in the nurse's words, and reluctantly got up to go. "My God, I don't have any money! My purse is in the car in the parking lot at Hanauma Bay. And yours is, too, Glynny. I didn't even think about it."

Glynnis reached into the bra of her bathing suit and unpinned a plastic pouch full of dollar bills. "I guess I'm always a little cautious. I was afraid to be totally without cash, even if we were in the water. It's not much, but it will get us through the day."

"Nice going, dear," the nurse nodded. "And if you run out, you just go to the admin office and tell them what's going on. I think they'll work something out. And if they won't, the other nurses and I will. By the way, my name is Leila. I'd like to help you."

"You're helping more than you can imagine, Leila. Thanks so much." Allison held out her hand and patted the nurse.

The line at the cafeteria was a strange combination. Staff personnel—doctors, nurses, office workers—blended with patients' families and visitors, most looking with blank faces, but sometimes laughing and talking. Several ambulatory patients were enjoying a snack away from their room. Most people smiled, but everyone seemed distant, with their minds on their own thoughts and troubles.

"Just think, with these bathrobes on, people probably think we're patients. Well, I feel pretty much like a basket case, so they're not far wrong. Y'know, I can't believe it, but this soup looks terrific. I hadn't even thought of eating, but I'm famished." Allison placed a roll on her tray along with her cup of soup. They paid and found a table. Glynnis unloaded her tray and sat down. "It's strange that your body knows what it needs, even if you forget. I have a craving for this turkey sandwich and hot tea."

A memory caused Allison to stop and smile. "Only once did I ever spent much time in a hospital—well, except to have the kids, and that doesn't count. I mean as a visitor. Joe's mother was ill and they sent her to the hospital in Anchorage. We flew over and stayed for several days. There was a dormitory that was part of the hospital, and people from out of town could stay there almost free of charge. We bought food and used the community kitchen to prepare our meals. It really helped out, and we were able to stay close to Beth, Joe's mother.

"What made me laugh just now, I remember that the path between our room and the main hospital went through a little garden. It was winter, so there were no leaves on the small trees, but hanging on all the bare limbs were bars of bath soap. Green. It was the weirdest thing I ever saw. One of the volunteers told us that the soap somehow discouraged the moose from eating the bark from the young trees. In the cold of winter they get pretty desperate, and were coming right into the hospital grounds to munch on whatever they could find. But they didn't like the odor of this brand of soap so they left the trees alone. Strange, huh?"

"During Mother's illness I stayed full-time there, too, and I began to notice a young woman who seemed to be in the corridor almost all the time. She was very thin and nervous and walked incessantly. I think you call it power walking. Very fast, and determined. She looked straight ahead, and her eyes were flushed, never really looking at anything. I thought it was odd, and felt so much compassion for her. I could never understand if she was a visitor who was simply trying to get some exercise, or if she was a patient. She seemed troubled, but then we were all troubled." Glynnis sighed. "But I watched her feverish activity as though I were watching a movie. Detached. When you're deeply concerned about someone you love, the rest of life takes on less importance, and sometimes becomes a little surreal."

"Yeah, well I'll tell you, this is pretty surreal." Allison paused, wishing she could stop her thoughts. "Glynnis, I'm really worried. I know we're sure that everything's going to be okay, but what if it's not? And what if Susan is all right, but . . . I don't even want to say it. I'm pretty scared."

"I know, Allison. I'm worried, too. But if we know we have done everything we can to help, it is more useful for us to focus on and expect the best than to worry about the worst. I believe we exert energy from our actions and emotions. We want to make sure we point it in the right direction. I will not conceive of anything but a good outcome."

"You're right. It's about all we can do, anyway. But I would like to get back up there. Ready?"

They took the elevator to the next floor and walked down the corridor toward Susan's room. Standing in the hallway was a figure Glynnis recognized immediately. "Timothy. Thank you for coming." He folded her in his arms, and then seeing Allison, held out his hand and held hers tightly.

"There's nothing I can tell you to help. But God, I'd give the world if I could change things. All I can do is be here. And I will do just that for as much time as I can, as long as it takes. Dear Lord, I wish there were something I could do. Are you all right, Allison?" He carefully eased Glynnis' arms away and held her at arms' length in order to study her face. "You look pretty rocky, Chopin. Are you going to be all right?"

"Now I will be. Hm. Chopin. That's nice." The three moved into the lounge area and were soon joined by a troubled Eric.

"I can't believe this. I want to know how it happened, but I'll wait until you feel like talking. You look beat." He explained he'd picked up the car at the beach. "Luckily, all the stuff in the trunk was still there. That's a pretty notorious place for guys to break into cars to rob you blind. But here's your purses, and whatever clothes were in the back. It looks like you could do with a change."

The hours passed sluggishly, livened only by an occasional trip to the cafeteria or coffee dispenser at the other end of the corridor. Everyone held a magazine in their hands, turning pages, but no one seemed to be reading. Now and then someone changed positions from one chair to another. The room was heavy with concern. The emergency room doctor who admitted Susan looked in on them regularly, but not often, and Leila and the other nurses tried to cheer them up and look after their needs. But the message was always the same. Susan remained unconscious, they were concerned about the loss of blood and possible internal injuries. Her vital signs remained fairly good. They wouldn't comment on the outlook for the baby. The women were allowed to look in on her and found her ashen and still. After only a few moments the nurse gently guided them out. The clock ticked on.

It grew late and Glynnis talked Timothy into going home for the night. Eric had gone earlier. Both promised they'd return in the morning. Leila brought blankets and both women tried to rest on the couches. Neither could sleep very well, but exhaustion won in the end, and each stole a few fitful hours of rest.

*Chapter Fourteen*
# Sunday

**They roused in** the early hours of the morning, awakened by hushed conversation in the corridor. Both got up quietly, checked the clock, and stretched, trying to rid their bodies of aches caused by the rigid confines of the small couches.

The voices were coming from a group in the center of the corridor in front of Susan's room. They recognized one of the doctors, but no one else. Allison reached for Glynnis' hand, worried, and they approached.

The ER doctor noticed them and greeted them wearily. He introduced the others. Susan's gynecologist, Dr. Liu was one of them. Their hearts broke a little more as they were introduced to Philip, who had arrived just after midnight. They had hardly been introduced when he cradled them both with his arms and cried. No one spoke.

Minutes passed, and Philip finally pulled away, his eyes now dry, his face somewhat composed. "Susan is going to be all right. Dr. Edwards just confirmed that she has no injuries that will have lasting effect. Very bruised and battered, but all in one piece. She regained consciousness a few minutes ago.

"The baby . . ." his body slumped and he couldn't go on.

Dr. Liu spoke up quietly. "It appears that Susan has lost the baby." Confronted with silence, he paused, then continued gently. "Apparently she received a severe blow to her abdomen while she was in the water, and the trauma has caused her to miscarry. There is not much I can say that will make that any less painful except that her condition would suggest that Susan can certainly have other children." He paused, looking at Philip, then the others. "I must go now. I'm very sorry. Call me if I can be of any help."

Philip struggled to speak. "I am so grateful that Sue will be all right. And I know that we will get through this. It's just that . . . it was such a gift, and now it's gone." Fighting to remain in control, he spoke quickly. "If you should go in to see Susan, she doesn't know yet. I'm about to tell her. Maybe you should wait awhile. She drifts in and out of sleep, and Dr. Edwards here tells me that rest is crucial. She's exhausted."

No one spoke, but Glynnis took Philip's hand and Allison put her arm around him. All were crying. Timothy walked down the corridor quietly and joined the solemn group.

"Susan is going to be okay. That's wonderful. We had just hoped that . . ." Allison couldn't finish.

"She is going to need you as never before, Philip. And you will find strength in Susan. Support each other, and you'll each draw courage from the other. You will both get through this." Glynnis spoke to Philip as though she were willing her words to comfort him.

Their conversation was cut short when they heard Susan calling for Phil.

Susan couldn't decide whether she was awake or sleeping. She had been somewhere very black, and in and out of dreams, for what seemed like days. She tried to touch her face, thinking if she could feel anything she would certainly be awake, but it was impossible to know if she had really moved her arm to touch her face or if it was simply her imagination.

How annoying that there were so many people in her room, but as they milled around she began to identify them one by one. Mother and Dad, Philip, friends and contemporaries, law professors, high school chums. Her first grade teacher, Miss Morgan. Everyone wanted her to join them in whatever they were doing. It occurred to her they were working very hard to entice her to abandon what she was thinking about and join them. But then Mother and Aunt Maureen were on the other side of her bed, away from the rest, and were speaking to her with much animation. As hard as she tried, it was impossible to understand their words. Tired, she tried to turn to the others and leave with her friends, but Mother and Maureen grasped her shoulders and stared forcefully into her eyes. She knew them well enough to realize they were trying desperately to help her in some way, but she was distracted and couldn't fathom their urgent looks.

Troubled, she tried to get Phil's attention, but he was talking to someone. Ah, it was Glynnis and Allison. They were here too, although she wasn't quite sure where "here" was. When he didn't hear her, she called even louder. They needed to do something. She simply had to concentrate hard enough to understand what it was.

"Sue, it's fine, I'm right here. I was just outside." Philip was alarmed to see her looking upset as he rushed in from the corridor.

It was hard to stay awake, but she needed to talk. "Darling, something's not right, and I've got to figure out what to do about it. It's important"

Drawing a deep breath, Philip dreaded what had to come next, but there was no retreating. He must tell her. He needed to be truthful with Susan. Always they told the truth to each other, even when it was bad news. "The doctor says you'll be fine, honey. You'll be 100 percent in no time. You just need to rest and get back some strength. But I have to tell you something else, and it will hurt. We've lost the baby. But Dr. Liu says you will be able to have other children. We'll just have to wait. It's okay. We'll be okay."

Susan didn't want to hear the words, but was powerless to stop them. Yet she had known anyway. Tears were streaming down her torn and swollen face, but she was too weak to say or do anything more. She wanted to lie there and simply give in. Just go back to sleep, it was too much. But Mother and Aunt Maureen were still there, looking her straight in the eye.

"NO!" Susan's eyes flew open, she screamed and tried to get up.

"You've got to relax, Susan. I know how tough this is, but we can't change it. We love each other, and we'll get through it together. I need your help, and I'll be here to help you, you can count on it." He smoothed her hair as he talked quietly.

"Phil, you weren't here, you don't understand." She stopped, reaching inward for more strength. "I've already gone through this, I hear what you're saying. It's hard to keep it in my mind. I understand about the miscarriage."

Susan closed her eyes again and Phil was grateful for the respite, however short it might be. Susan was in a fragile state and this was agony for him. He held her hands in his, head bent down.

After some moments she roused, agitated. "But I still have the baby. I know it." Even through tears, her voice was determined.

"Oh, Sue, if only I could change this I would. But it's something we're just going to face together. Look, you should rest now. We'll talk more later."

"It's the only time I <u>can</u> worry about it. It's crucial. Don't you understand? I don't even have time to grieve right now. I know it would be impossible for anybody else to comprehend it. I've been in and out of dreams and slipped off into places I've never been before. But something came through very clearly. I'm pregnant. I know I am. It's not the first time I've known things at this level. Intuition, or whatever. Mother is like that, too. Perhaps more than me. I'm very tired, but I know I have to do something about this. Maybe you can help me. Do you believe me?"

"Susan, whatever you want me to do, I'll do it."

"Go find Dr. Liu. I have to talk to him."

The mixture of emotions in the waiting room was difficult. Susan was going to be fine. Glynnis and Allison had seen her battered body transported from the ragged coastline just hours before, and this was the outcome they had prayed for. But the baby! Sue and Philip had surmounted difficult hurdles, and their baby was going to fill their lives. They remembered her expression of love and joy when she told them of her upcoming marriage and keeping the baby. Despite all her quiet dignity, Susan had looked like a young child cherishing a most wonderful gift.

They'd shared her elation to the fullest. Now they must share her loss. It was hard to know how to begin the long journey through grief. Their tired faces reflected the bitterness of the moment.

Timothy looked at Glynnis' eyes, red from lack of sleep and tears, and gently stood her up. "You and I are going out somewhere for breakfast. You have to get away from here."

"Oh, no. I can't do that, Tim. Susan may need me, or Philip. I must stay here."

"I know you need a break. I won't let you stay, no matter what I have to do to get you to go with me. I'll bring you right back, I promise. Just come away and breathe some fresh air for an hour or two. I don't want to be mean, but I'm not letting you say no."

"Listen to the man, Glyn. If it makes you feel less worried, Eric phoned and is coming to get me so I can go to the apartment and take a hot shower and change. And I'll bring you fresh clothes, too. We both need to get away. My heart tells me to stay here, but I know Phil wants time with Sue, and maybe being anywhere but here will help me remember there's a real world out there. We'll both come back soon, and can start in where we left off. Wherever that is."

Timothy agreed with Allison and suggested they meet at the apartment so Glynnis could also shower and freshen up, then drive back to the hospital together. Reluctantly, Glynnis left. Sad and worried as she was, the warmth of Timothy's arm around her gladdened her heart. He drove her to a small cafe where they ordered breakfast. When he asked her when she last ate, Glynnis realized it had been the sandwich yesterday afternoon.

"I feel so helpless. There should be something I could do, something to say to make this better. But there's nothing. I can't change a thing."

"You're so mistaken, maestro. Of course you can't change

fate, you couldn't save Susan's baby or make the accident go away. But you were there, waiting and worrying, making sure the doctors were doing the right thing. You told them about the baby. They would probably not have known if it hadn't have been for you."

"What good did it do. The baby is dead. I wanted Susan to have her baby, and I wanted to be an auntie. To be part of a that little baby's life."

"Don't beat yourself up like this. That's out of your control. But let me tell you something I know about you. You've often confided in me that you were not as bold or strong as others. Well, in a sense, that's true. You're more shy than you are aggressive, and I admire you for that quality. You are gentle and sweet, and wouldn't hurt anyone or anything. But I've seen you stand up for your friend during this long time with incredible strength. You took charge when you had to. You've been remarkable. I've watched you with the doctors. I heard you talk to Phil a while ago, and I could see how it helped, your strength rallied his spirit.

"And I know something even more about you. Dad wrote to me when your father died. He was full of admiration for what you went through with your mother and then your father so soon after. He said you practically lived in the hospital, rarely going home. You put shyness aside when it came to talking to the doctors, keeping track of what needed to be done, making critical decisions. You shielded both your parents from sometimes detached and impersonal encounters with doctors and nurses. Dad told me he saw you once look a young intern in the eye and tell him, politely but firmly, that your father was wide awake in the bed, and if questions needed to be answered, they were to be addressed to him. You informed him he was not to ask you, 'Did he sleep well last night?' when your father was perfectly capable of answering the question. My dad said you would not allow this young kid to talk about your father as though he were a specimen in a bottle. That takes sensitivity, which you have plenty of, but it also takes guts, and you're not wanting for those when you need them."

"I can't believe Uncle John felt that I did anything other than just care for both of them as they needed to be cared for."

"He recognized the difference between simply doing what was necessary and caring to the fullest about your parents' feelings and wellbeing."

Glynnis displayed the first hint of a smile in many long hours. "I really like your father."

"My father and I regard you very highly, too, sweet Glynnis." And I see you're blushing, so that must mean it matters at least a little to you. I hope so." Timothy smiled and held her hand.

"Thank you for bringing me here. I needed to get away, and seeing you was the best medicine. But I think we should go on to the apartment. By the time I have a shower and we get back, we will have been away a long time."

"I could argue with you, but I won't. You do what you have to do, and I'll try to keep my white horse saddled so I can ride in and save you every time you're ready to collapse from hunger. We Hawaiians place a lot of importance on eating well, and it doesn't make sense to us to go without a meal. That's what keeps you strong and beautiful. That's what Alesa told me! Come on, we'll get going."

Glynnis made her time at the apartment as short as possible, though the relaxing shower tempted her to prolong it.

She gathered up some useful items and soon Tim was driving her and Allison back to the hospital.

"I want to go back to be near Sue, but I really dread going back in those doors, you know what I mean?" Allison gazed out the window.

"I know, I feel the same way. But it will be okay." Glynnis hesitated a moment, then turned to Timothy. "I've made up my mind about Alesa's offer. I'll call her tonight, of course, and talk to her about it, but I want you to know that I've decided to stay awhile with her. I said before that I had to get back to take care of business, but there's nothing I can't take care of from here. In fact, the most important thing I have to consider now is what to do with the rest of my life, and perhaps this is the best place to do it." She stopped, a bit off-balance. "This might be the best place to do it because I've been able to think so clearly, and I've learned to deal with things in a different way. It has inspired me, I suppose. I'm afraid when I return to Philadelphia the old habits will soon find me, and I'll turn into the old me. I'm going to take more time to find myself.

"And Alesa is a special treasure that has come into my life. I mustn't just leave and never see her again. I need time with her."

"And what about more time with me?" Timothy looked at her gravely. "I am not going to joke about this, Chopin. You're very important to me. I don't want to let go of you so soon, and I hope you feel the same about me."

Glynnis spoke quietly. "I do want to spend more time with you, Tim. You have become very special to me." She smiled and tried to lighten the mood. "And I need to make sure you practice that piano regularly!"

"Whoa, guys, you mean you're staying right here, Glyn? No more Philadelphia?"

"I didn't say that. I am going to extend my time here, though. Don't put words in my mouth, Allison!" Glynnis smiled at her good friend.

"Me? I wouldn't think of butting in. You know me!"

They arrived at the hospital. Timothy parked and the three suddenly became quiet. It was hard to face reality again, and they felt small and lonely as they went up to Susan's floor.

The moment they stepped out of the elevator it was apparent something was changed. There was too much noise. Glynnis grabbed hold of Timothy and Allison, frightened. They walked to the nurse' station, where the duty nurse was humming as she worked. "Could you tell us how Miss Michaels is doing? Has she been resting?" Allison looked toward Susan's room, anxiously.

The nurse opened her mouth to reply, but thought better of it as she saw Philip approaching. "I shouldn't be the one to tell you. Here's Mr. Alexander. He'll explain."

Philip caught sight of them and ran over. His face was transformed. He was happy. "Susan has a baby. I mean, she is still pregnant. You're not going to believe this miracle. We're going to have a baby!"

Tim held up his hands to slow things down. Hey, Phil, this has been a hard day for you."

"Yeah, but you won't believe what's happened." He stopped for a moment, seeing the puzzled looks and realizing he hadn't explained anything to them. "Susan has always been pretty eerie about her intuition. Says she gets it from Peggy, her mother. But it's frightening, almost, how often she's right about things.

When she called for me this morning and I left you to go to her room, she was pretty out of it, but I told her what she had to hear. That she had miscarried. It was tough on her. She kept sinking back into sleep, then rousing up, and out again. But what she was saying didn't make much sense. She was fighting with something inside her, struggling to do something. I thought she was just destroyed because of the baby.

"She finally worked through it herself enough to get me to call Dr. Liu, the OB/GYN. When he came back she was adamant that she was still pregnant. She told us she realized the baby was gone. She couldn't understand how it could be, but she simply knew she still had a child.

"I expected Dr. Liu to give her a sedative or something, but instead he pondered a minute, and then ordered some tests. He told me later he ran those tests because he knew that Susan was a professional used to dealing with facts, and he hoped if he showed her valid test results she would respect them and it would convince her of the truth, however unbearable." Philip beamed. "But you know what? She IS pregnant. The doctor explained to us that she had been carrying twins. He had heard of this happening before. It's not rare, but it is uncommon. One baby aborts, for whatever reason, but the other is left intact. In Sue's case, the severe blow to her stomach caused fatal injuries to one fetus. The other one was protected and survived." Phil was crying. "Susan has been waiting to see you. Want to go in?"

Susan was propped up in her bed, still a terrible picture of bruises and cuts, but smiling broadly. Bouquets covered every free space in the room. Philip had seemingly bought every available flower in Honolulu. "Oh, Allison, Glynnis. I couldn't wait for you to get here so we could tell you. Can you believe this gift! This morning was the worst thing to ever happen to me, and it was even worse because Phil was suffering just as much. I don't know how to explain this, because we are grieving for the baby that we lost, but God has given us another. It's not that it will replace the one we lost. Nothing will. But we will cherish this little survivor so much. I'll never be able to do enough to merit this gift. But I will try my hardest."

Speechless for a moment, they were silent as the incredible story finally sank in. And then the group celebrated, laughter and tears intermixed in equal proportions. They celebrated until a sympathetic but concerned doctor told them they should let Susan rest. As happy as they all were, it had been a rough day. Grinning broadly, they acknowledged that the party should come to an end.

"I guess Glynnis and I will head back to the apartment for the night. Philip, where are you staying?"

"Nobody can get me away from here. I'll be fine. I don't want to let this lady out of my sight. And by the way, the doctor thinks I can take her back to San Francisco in a couple of days. We'll just bundle her up and move her from her bed here to a hospital bed in San Francisco. She's not going to do much else but relax for quite awhile."

Susan spoke up. "I guess I'm not going to see much more of you two women. Allison, I've already messed up your schedule, and Glynnis, you must be thinking about heading home."

"I didn't think I'd be reconstructing my travel plans this soon, but maybe I will try to get out day after tomorrow. I think I'm going to sleep through tomorrow!" Allison's eyes twinkled. "Allison, tell Sue about the monumental changes in your plans.

"Not monumental. Just temporary. Susan, as you know Alesa has asked me to stay on awhile, and I've decided to accept her wonderful invitation. Now I'm even more glad I'm staying. I'll be able to keep an eye on you until you're able to leave in a few days. Of course, Philip is doing a pretty remarkable job all by himself. But I'll come over and we can visit. Timothy too, perhaps." Glynnis' eyes shone with enthusiasm.

"There's just one thing I want to say before I lose the chance." Allison's voice betrayed the sadness she felt at leaving her friends. "This has been a time for me that's like nothing I've ever experienced before. So much has happened to us all, and look what a short time we've known each other. Let's not let it just die out. Why don't we plan to get together in a year. An anniversary! Can we all come right back here?"

"I love the idea. We'll have our baby, and it will be just the right time to introduce him or her to Hawaii. Does it sound possible to you, Glynnis?"

"I agree. I couldn't bear the thought of not seeing you both again. I'll look forward to our reunion all year. Of course I can come over again next year."

"You're not planning to leave any time soon are you, maestro? You may still be here." He paused. "Helping Alesa." Tim laughed, expecting an argument. None came.

The party broke up, Glynnis and Allison promising they'd return tomorrow.

*Chapter Fifteen*
# Monday

**They woke next** morning to rain, and although they were still elated about the baby, it was difficult to work through the day of packing up getting ready to leave the apartment. Alesa had insisted Glynnis move right over and invited Allison to spend that night with her so Tim could take her to the airport the next morning. Several times through the morning they stopped to take last looks at this or that, to enjoy Noelani's unforgettable breakfast one last time. Good-byes were said. Eric promised he'd try to make it to Alaska to meet Joe and learn about salmon fishing.

They spent the rest of the day with Susan, helping her get ready for a careful trip to California. She was surprised by an impromptu wedding/baby shower that Glynnis and Allison had put together on short notice. A few gifts and a small cake. A bottle of champagne was chilled and brought in and they toasted everything, Susan substituting sparkling apple cider. Nurses and doctors filed in as they had time, anxious to share in the festivities and still marveling at the unbelievable chain of events. Timothy brought Alesa, who presented Susan with a sketch of the three women, done from her memory of the dinner party they so recently enjoyed.

The afternoon turned to evening, and they knew they must leave. Sad to part, but each happy for the others, they embraced and promised letters, gave last minute advice and related countless times how much they cared for each other. But it had to end. The three held hands quietly and swore they'd be back together in a year's time.

It was time to move on.

*Chapter Sixteen*

# Tuesday

**The car nudged** into a free space outside the departure area of Honolulu International Airport, and Timothy unloaded Allison's bags onto a cart. "I'll park and meet you two inside," he shouted as he headed toward the airport garage.

Glynnis and Allison maneuvered through the throngs of people to the ticket counter, where Allison checked her bags. Here they were again, two young women in this balmy airport, so recently strangers, but now solid friends. Warm tropical air, the wild scent of flowers, happy people scurrying in all directions became a surrealistic scene to Allison as they retraced their steps of such a short time ago. Preparing to leave Hawaii and return to her home and family, there was joy in her heart, yet new bonds of love encased her heart. Part of her now belonged to this place. It would always be in her mind, her heart. Within a handful of days on this Island her emotions had been pulled back from the edge of despair to a new level of understanding and love. People had happened into her life in the casualness of a chance meeting, and now they were firmly woven into the pattern and meaning of her future. She guessed this was what it must be like to be shipwrecked or to be held hostage with strangers. You share something with them that no one else understands. These three had come off the airplane into this airport as total strangers, bundled in their privacy, each at a precarious point in their lives, and through an intricate web of events something had come about, something illusive but important. Their relationship was much deeper than a casual, ten-day friendship. And the strength of this bond helped them to break out toward an unexplored horizon full of promise, adding a fuller, broader aspect to their lives. Allison tried to convey these thoughts to Glynnis.

"You know, Eve was fashioned from Adam's rib to give him company, and to me that means comfort and support. Life can be difficult at times, and it's hard to go it alone. You need somebody on your side. Well, in a way, we three women fashioned that same thing for each other. Eve's rib, I guess you could call it. Funny way to forge a friendship, but it sure gave us more strength to do what needed to be done. We weren't out there alone. Somebody else cared, and it helped a lot."

"I feel more like the Cowardly Lion, who finally got Courage," Glynnis smiled and sighed. "You and Susan had such heartbreaking problems to work through, but you were both secure, well-rounded people. I needed a total make-over, so if finding two wonderful friends did that for me, I'm a lucky girl. So lucky." She hesitated, then continued, "Tim has taught me a lot about Hawaii and why it is so special to him. Of course, there is such beauty here, it's easy to see why you'd fall in love with it, but there's more than that. It's hard for me to understand completely, Tim calls it the spirit of Aloha. He explained that Hawaiians feel very close to those they love; they are part of you, and you are part of them. If you are hurt, they are hurt, and they are joyful in your happiness. There is honor and respect for the land and the people, and they feel a responsibility to be worthy of the gift they've been given. It's an endearing quality, and I think somehow we were given that gift of the Aloha spirit when we all landed in Hawaii."

"I love it, Glynny!" Allison sobered. "But here I am, thrilled to be on my way home, yet in spite of that, it's hard to go. I can't stand leaving you and all that's become so important to me here. I'm going to miss you so much, Glynnis. When that plane takes off, it's really going to hurt!" She wiped tears from her face and tried to smile.

Soberly, but with a new assurance, Glynnis hugged Allison. "There's so much I should say to you, Allison. You saved my life. Really, you did. And because of you I am starting out on a great new adventure. I'm excited, no, thrilled! Life is different now, and you did it for me. I dread seeing you go. But I know it's going to be okay. And we will all carry a little piece of each other within us, in that Aloha spirit." She looked hopefully at Allison. "You will come back next year, won't you?"

"Same time next year! We've all three promised." Allison smiled warmly, reassuring herself at the same time that this good-bye was not forever. "Maybe Joe and the kids can come with me, and Susan will come with Phil and their new baby!"

Timothy broke through the crowds to join them and the three walked on toward the gates. As they left the main lobby, Glynnis excused herself and came back moments later with a lei of white tuberose and fern which she placed over Allison's shoulders. More tears flowed as Glynnis kissed her friend's cheek. "Aloha. Come back soon to this lovely land."

They all knew it was time for Allison to leave. She hugged Glynnis tightly, vowing solemnly she'd be back in a year. Timothy promised he'd look after Glyn and wished Allison a safe trip home. She turned and melted into the line of boarding passengers. Before passing through the security gate, she turned to wave one more time and her heart overflowed with happiness as she saw Timothy put his arm around Glynnis to comfort her, and then kiss her on the forehead. Even from a distance she could feel the warmth between them. *She's going to be all right. I just know it. That's a marriage in the making if I ever saw one!*

*Well, old girl, things have worked out pretty well for all of us. Susan is going to be all right, even though they lost a baby. But the miracle baby is out of danger, she and Phil are about to be married, and now her career is not the only thing in her life. It's so much richer now. Glynnis beat the odds by changing gears a little to let herself dare to be more than a wallflower. I hope I had a little to do with that transformation. Makes me feel good to think so, anyway. But imagine how her father reached out after his death to bring her insight and strength. What a brave man.*

*And here I am, the old Alaskan, going back to the man I love, the children I cherish. So I didn't make any drastic changes. I didn't have to. I will happily forego drama and excitement for the steadiness and love Joe and I have together. And when I'm old I'll look back on this escapade and laugh at myself. I'm glad I did it, though. It made me think straight, and Joe, too, and brought me two wonderful, dear friends. Plus, if I'm lucky, I'll keep this tan all summer long!*

With her head full of thoughts, Allison worked her to the gate and soon was boarding, making her way through the crowded plane and locating her assigned window seat. The aisle seat was already occupied by a fellow studying a newspaper, blanket pulled all around him, covering even his face. *Seems like he's asleep, but I've got to get in there.* Allison hated to disturb the man, but people were waiting for her to move out of their way.

"Hey, I'm sorry sir. I hate to bother you, but I have the window seat." She tried to inch past him quickly to clear the aisle, and eased down into her seat. Odd that this guy should be so bundled up and even asleep since he must have boarded only moments before her. Well, you never know. Probably had too many mai tais in the airport bar saying alohas. *Hoo boy. This could be a long trip. He'd better not be a sloppy drunk or get aggressive. I'll pitch him out into the aisle.*

As she got comfortable and arranged carry-on items, her seatmate roused and pulled the blanket down from around his face. She carefully avoided looking toward him, but suddenly he leaned over and spoke in a loud, husky voice that everyone around them could hear, "I've been waiting all my life to have a pretty dame like you sit beside me in an airplane. What took you so long?"

Startled and irritated, Allison looked over at this annoying person. All at once she gasped, not believing what she saw. "Joe? Joe! How—what—you can't be here!" The two threw their arms around each other as passengers all over the plane tried to understand exactly what had just happened.

A stern looking woman directly behind them clucked disapprovingly. "Disgusting" Her traveling companion tapped her purse impatiently on her knees." I just don't know what this world is coming to, Lorraine."Two youngsters across the aisle giggled.

Unfazed by the commotion they were causing, Allison gestured wildly. "How did you get here? How long have you been in Hawaii? Oh, I love you so much! I can't believe this is happening."

"Well, Sonny, I got to thinking about our life. Everything considered, it's a damned good life, and we're going to keep it just the way it is, except for one thing. I'm not taking anything for granted anymore. I figure you need some special handling now and then, like my planes, sort of, and this is one of those times. I took the red-eye flight from Anchorage last night. Got into Honolulu early this morning and roamed around the airport for a few hours. One of my buddies back home introduced me to the pilot, and when I told him what I wanted, he arranged for me board real early so I'd avoid running into you before you got on, and I've been holed up in here waiting for you. It seemed like a lifetime. God, you're beautiful, Sonny." He stroked her hair as he talked.

"I'm speechless, Joe. I can't believe you planned this whole thing. What about our planes, the business? What about our place? Who's looking after everything? Do the children know where you are? Did you tell Mom and Dad?

"Be quiet, honey. I'm the worrier, remember? I took care of everything. Just seemed like the thing to do." Joe was beaming as he watched his wife's amazement. "Look, I even dressed up just for you!"

As her mind adjusted to the shock of all this, Allison noticed that he was wearing that abominable fishing shirt, but there was something different about it. It took a minute to realize that he had starched and ironed it. Raveling around the collar, second button missing, pocket a little torn away from the shirt at one corner, stains from cleaning long-forgotten fish arrayed like prized medals, but impeccably stiff and pressed. "As I recall, I owe you a night on the town because of this shirt." He tried to be serious.

"You are the most wonderful man in the world. I can't wait to get you home and alone—after the kids are asleep, that is."

"Well, that'll be a while, my dear. You see, we're going to Seattle, check on the kids, and then I have reservations at one of the greatest hotels in town for just you and me. I've talked with your folks, and they're all set with a million plans with the kids. So it'll be dinner out tonight for us at your favorite spot, and then two or three days all to ourselves. Nothing to do except . . . see the sights." Joe winked devilishly at his wife, pulling her closer as he kissed her. He noticed that almost everyone in the plane was staring at them by now, no doubt intrigued and amazed at his forwardness and quick moves on a perfect stranger. He stood to address them. "She's my wife. Can you beat that! And she still loves me." There was a hearty round of applause from around the cabin. Allison waved happily, then turned to Joe.

"You say we're going to spend two or three days? I'm betting we just may not have enough time to see any sights. Allison sobered. "What would I do without you, Joe."

He laughed, "I like that a lot better than 'what will I do <u>with</u> you! But how about giving me some warning next time you want to go off and leave me."

"No way, my friend. Keep 'em guessing, that's my style. Besides, I love the way you make it all work out in the end." Allison had never felt happier, more loved, more sure of Joe. *But don't kid yourself, my girl. Enjoy this, because I'll bet this kind of chivalry is going to come around once every blue moon, at most.*

She settled her head against Joe's shoulder. "Want to know a secret? I really love that damned shirt."

CPSIA information can be obtained at www.ICGtesting.com
Printed in the USA
BVOW071904231012

303750BV00001B/42/P

9 781432 797560